BROOM SERVICE

SEA WITCH COZY MYSTERIES BOOK 5

MORGANA BEST

Broom Service
Sea Witch Cozy Mysteries Book 5
Copyright © 2020 by Morgana Best
All rights reserved.
ISBN 9780648660149

No part of this book may be reproduced in any form or by any electronic or mechanical means, including information storage and retrieval systems, without written permission from the author, except for the use of brief quotations in a book review.

This is a work of fiction. Any resemblance to any person, living or dead, is purely coincidental. The personal names have been invented by the author, and any likeness to the name of any person, living or dead, is purely coincidental.

This book may contain references to specific commercial products, process or service by trade name, trademark, manufacturer, or otherwise, specific brand-name products and/or trade names of products, which are trademarks or registered trademarks and/or trade names, and these are property of their respective owners. Morgana Best or her associates, have no association with any specific commercial products, process, or service by trade name, trademark, manufacturer, or otherwise, specific brand-name products and / or trade names of products.

GLOSSARY

*S*ome Australian spellings and expressions are entirely different from US spellings and expressions. Below are just a few examples.

It would take an entire book to list all the differences.

For example, people often think "How are you going?" (instead of "How are you doing?") is an error, but it's normal and correct for Aussies!

The author has used Australian spelling in this series. Here are a few examples: *Mum* instead of the US spelling *Mom*, *neighbour* instead of the US spelling *neighbor*, *realise* instead of the US spelling *realize*. It is *Ms*, *Mr* and *Mrs* in Australia, not *Ms.*, *Mr.* and *Mrs.*; *defence* not *defense;* *judgement* not *judg-*

ment; *cosy* and not *cozy*; *1930s* not *1930's*; *offence* not *offense*; *centre* not *center*; *towards* not *toward*; *jewellery* not *jewelry*; *favour* not *favor*; *mould* not *mold*; *two storey house* not *two story house*; *practise* (verb) not *practice* (verb); *odour* not *odor*; *smelt* not *smelled*; *travelling* not *traveling*; *liquorice* not *licorice*; *cheque* not *check*; *leant* not *leaned*; *have concussion* not *have a concussion*; *anti clockwise* not *counterclockwise*; *go to hospital* not *go to the hospital*; *sceptic* not *skeptic*; *aluminium* not *aluminum*; *learnt* not *learned*. We have *fancy dress* parties not *costume* parties. We don't say *gotten*. We say *car crash* (or *accident*) not *car wreck*. We say *a herb* not *an herb* as we pronounce the 'h.'

The above are just a few examples.

It's not just different words; Aussies sometimes use different expressions in sentence structure. We might *eat a curry* not *eat curry*. We might say *in the main street* not *on the main street*. Someone might be *going well* instead of *doing well*. We might say *without drawing breath* not *without drawing a breath*.

These are just some of the differences.

Please note that these are not mistakes or typos, but correct, normal Aussie spelling, terms, and syntax.

AUSTRALIAN SLANG AND TERMS

Benchtops - counter tops (kitchen)
Big Smoke - a city
Blighter - infuriating or good-for-nothing person
Blimey! - an expression of surprise
Bloke - a man (usually used in nice sense, "a good bloke")
Blue (noun) - an argument ("to have a blue")
Bluestone - copper sulphate (copper sulfate in US spelling)
Bluo - a blue laundry additive, an optical brightener
Boot (car) - trunk (car)
Bonnet (car) - hood (car)
Bore - a drilled water well
Budgie smugglers (variant: budgy smugglers) - named after the Aussie native bird, the budgerigar. A slang term for brief and tight-fitting men's swimwear
Bugger! - as an expression of surprise, not a swear word
Bugger - as in "the poor bugger" - refers to an unfortunate person (not a swear word)
Bunging it on - faking something, pretending

Bush telegraph - the grapevine, the way news spreads by word of mouth in the country
Car park - parking lot
Cark it - die
Chooks - chickens
Come good - turn out okay
Copper, cop - police officer
Coot - silly or annoying person
Cream bun - a sweet bread roll with copious amounts of cream, plus jam (= jelly in US) in the centre
Crook - 1. "Go crook (on someone)" - to berate them. 2. (someone is) crook - (someone is) ill. 3. Crook (noun) - a criminal
Demister (in car) - defroster
Drongo - an idiot
Dunny - an outhouse, a toilet, often ramshackle
Fair crack of the whip - a request to be fair, reasonable, just
Flannelette (fabric) - cotton, wool, or synthetic fabric, one side of which has a soft finish.
Flat out like a lizard drinking water - very busy
Galah - an idiot
Garbage - trash
G'day - Hello
Give a lift (to someone) - give a ride (to someone)

Goosebumps - goose pimples
Gumboots - rubber boots, wellingtons
Knickers - women's underwear
Laundry (referring to the room) - laundry room
Lamingtons - iconic Aussie cakes, square, sponge, chocolate-dipped, and coated with desiccated coconut. Some have a layer of cream and strawberry jam (= jelly in US) between the two halves.
Lift - elevator
Like a stunned mullet - very surprised
Mad as a cut snake - either insane or very angry
Mallee bull (as fit as, as mad as) - angry and/or fit, robust, super strong.
Miles - while Australians have kilometres these days, it is common to use expressions such as, "The road stretched for miles," "It was miles away."
Moleskins - woven heavy cotton fabric with suede-like finish, commonly used as working wear, or as town clothes
Mow (grass / lawn) - cut (grass / lawn)
Neenish tarts - Aussie tart. Pastry base. Filling is based on sweetened condensed milk mixture or mock cream. Some have layer of raspberry jam (jam = jelly in US). Topping is in two equal halves: icing (= frosting in US), usually chocolate

on one side, and either lemon or pink on the other.

Pub - The pub at the south of a small town is often referred to as the 'bottom pub' and the pub at the north end of town, the 'top pub.' The size of a small town is often judged by the number of pubs - i.e. "It's a three pub town."

Red cattle dog - (variant: blue cattle dog usually known as a 'blue dog') - referring to the breed of Australian Cattle Dog. However, a 'red dog' is usually a red kelpie (another breed of dog)

Shoot through - leave

Shout (a drink) - to buy a drink for someone

Skull (a drink) - drink a whole drink without stopping

Stone the crows! - an expression of surprise

Takeaway (food) - Take Out (food)

Toilet - also refers to the room if it is separate from the bathroom

Torch - flashlight

Tuck in (to food) - to eat food hungrily

Ute / Utility - pickup truck

Vegemite - Australian food spread, thick, dark brown

Wardrobe - closet

Windscreen - windshield

Indigenous References

Bush tucker - food that occurs in the Australian bush

Koori - the original inhabitants/traditional custodians of the land of Australia in the part of NSW in which this book is set. *Murri* are the people just to the north. White European culture often uses the term, *Aboriginal people*.

CHAPTER 1

Detective Max Grayson fished his stepmother out of a jasmine bush. I enjoyed the view of Max's bottom in his very tight, very serious detective jeans—obviously not issued by the police force, because they were criminal—but I enjoyed the view.

My pet wombat and witch familiar, Persnickle, the fuzzy little beast, the marsupial who would give the hounds of hell a run for their money in the naughty department, had charged at Max's stepmother the moment she stepped out of her Jaguar, knocking her out of her orthopaedic shoes. It's not that Persnickle hated stepmothers, although he did love fairy-tale films, in which stepmothers got a bit of bad press, it's that he hated the colour orange.

The origin of this dislike had thus far eluded the pet psychologist I had enlisted to help Persnickle process his hatred. Who hated the colour orange? Not many people. But then, Persnickle wasn't a person.

"Keep that beast away from me!" Tabitha howled, as Max plucked a jasmine petal out of her bright orange hair.

"He was just saying hello," I said desperately as Persnickle started to nibble on the woman's ankle. "You didn't tell me you had orange, um, I mean red, hair."

Tabitha nudged Persnickle away with her foot and climbed onto the hood of her Jaguar. "I didn't know one needed to announce one's hair colour in order to gain entry into House Bloom," she shrieked.

If she kept carrying on this way, she wouldn't need to worry about Persnickle attacking her. She would have ripped all her hair out. "Get that rodent away from me!" she added in a booming howl.

"He's just being friendly," Oleander protested.

When Max had gently broken the news to me

that his father, stepmother, and mother were coming to town, I had stress-purchased five pairs of Jimmy Choos shoes (none of them orange) and a Chanel handbag. I didn't know how I was going to pay the bills now, but I did know I was going to look very cute.

Oleander and Athanasius had taken pity on me when I turned up to their retirement home in a new pair of shoes for the fifth time in a week.

"She's got another new pair of Jimmy Choos," Oleander had said to Athanasius after she had put in her dentures.

"Eihrnfa ejjehhe hjfa," Athanasius had replied, because he hadn't put his dentures in yet.

Oleander had turned to me and said, "Don't worry, dear. We'll do our best to help."

And they had. That morning, Oleander and Athanasius broke out of the retirement home. Of course, they didn't need to break out. The retirement home wasn't a prison. But Oleander had told me she had been up to some mischief and needed some respite from it. She didn't name the type of mischief, but she had that mischievous part in common with Persnickle. At least, she hadn't charged at Max's stepmother, sending her flying.

When I got Persnickle under control, Tabitha

leant down from the Jaguar, her face as orange as her hair. "You must be Goldie." Tabitha offered Oleander her hand.

Max's ears turned pink. "No, Tabby. That's Oleander. She's a dear friend of Goldie's and mine. *This* is Goldie." He nodded to me. I was in the garden, gripping Persnickle's leash for dear life.

Tabitha looked at me. "Surely, this is the maid?"

"I—no? It's nice to meet you," I lied, walking over to shake her hand. "Would you like to come inside?"

"Not until that little beast is locked in a cage."

I sighed. "Athanasius, would you mind taking Persnickle inside for a treat?"

"Eihrnfa ejjehhe hjfa," Athanasius replied, because he still hadn't put in his dentures yet.

After Persnickle was inside, Tabitha climbed inelegantly off the car and pulled down her skirt. She had Dolly Parton hair—although it was orange—and a bosom that spilled out of her pencil dress. She was eighty-two, and her entire face was frozen from an apparent overdose of Botox. It's a wonder she could speak.

"Your father has gone to the airport to collect that woman," Tabitha told Max.

I frowned. "What woman?"

"My mother," Max replied.

"Yes, apparently Delilah is too good to catch a taxi. Your father sent me ahead like I'm some common scout in a war movie." Tabitha shrugged off her faux fur coat and tossed it over my head.

I didn't know what was more confusing—the fact Tabitha was wearing a faux fur coat in the Australian summer, or the fact Tabitha thought of me as a coat rack. Sure, I had lost a little bit of weight recently, but not *that* much weight.

Oleander rescued me from it. "I'll hang this up and see what Athanasius is doing."

"I'll join you," Tabitha said. "Just go on ahead, would you, and make sure the giant rat is locked away safely."

Max and I found ourselves standing alone in her garden. "She's…" I began, but I didn't know how to finish that sentence, not politely, at any rate.

"She's a lot, yeah," Max conceded. "She's around twenty years older than my dad."

"Wait! Your dad left your mum for a woman twenty years older than him?"

Max exhaled a lungful of air and wrapped an arm around my shoulders. "My father always was an unusual man. He attended every single one of my soccer games. Every single one."

I frowned. "Is that bad?"

"No, but it's not very dad-like, is it? He was always there for me, always happy to give emotional support."

"Maybe, he's not your real dad?" I said playfully.

"I've always had my suspicions."

"Here's my husband now." Tabitha flew out of the house as another Jaguar pulled up to the curb. Just how many luxury cars did these people own? "And your mother, Maxwell. Goldie, I do hope you have hidden all the silver."

"I don't have any silver."

"Ah, so Delilah has been here before."

"What—no—she's not stolen anything from me?"

"Not yet."

Delilah was the exact opposite of Tabitha. She drifted out of the car and pulled me into a tight hug, only releasing me when Max cleared his throat.

"Maxy," Delilah cried. "You're too skinny."

"I've actually packed on a little bit of weight," Max said, his tone self-conscious.

Jack Grayson stepped from the Jaguar. "Nonsense. Grayson men have always been hunks. We were the original Hemsworths."

Jack looked nothing like his son. He was short and stick-thin, with jet-black hair and tortoiseshell-rimmed glasses. He was more a first-movie Harry Potter than a Hemsworth brother. I tried to imagine Tabitha and Delilah fighting over such a tiny man, but the idea only made me chuckle.

"Goldie, we've heard so much about you. You finally let my boy kiss you, hey?" Jack chuckled as he clapped me on the back.

Delilah winked at me. "Honestly, Jacky-boy, don't embarrass our son."

"I didn't!" Jack protested. "It's not like I told Goldie that Max slept in our bed until he was seven. Or that he insisted on sleeping with the light on in the hall until he was fifteen, because he was terrified of Santa."

Max's ears turned red. "I don't know why you were all so relaxed about a strange man sneaking into our house at night."

"He was bringing presents," Delilah said with a grin.

"You always warned me about accepting presents from strange men," Max countered.

I interrupted the laughter to say, "Dinner is almost ready."

I ushered everyone into the dining room. I hoped the dinner would go smoothly, and I was relieved to see Persnickle had fallen asleep in front of the television. If he woke up, I could put on a *Starsky and Hutch* episode for him, and that was guaranteed to keep him quiet. No, I thought Persnickle would be the least of my worries.

I hurried to the fridge and returned with two bottles of champagne. "Bubbly anyone?" I asked.

Before anyone could answer, there was an urgent knock on my front door. Through the frosted glass, I could see the outline of a tall figure.

I swung around, catching Max's glance as I did so. Surely, his father didn't have any more ex-wives? I hurried to the door and opened it. There, standing on the porch, was a uniformed cop.

"Detective Grayson, there's been a death!"

CHAPTER 2

A collective gasp went up from the table. Max hurried over to my side at the door. "Murder?"

The cop scratched his head. "It doesn't seem so. But given who it is, Constable Clancy sent me to fetch you."

I could feel Max tense beside me. "Who is it?"

"Sheila McFeeler."

I heard heavy breathing and looked behind me. Tabitha was standing there. "Sheila McFeeler?" she shrieked, wiping her hand through her unruly orange hair. "It's bad enough to speak ill of the dead, let alone mock them! Use the poor dead woman's real name, if you would be so kind."

She really was the most obnoxious woman. I took a deep breath. "Sheila McFeeler *is* her real name," I explained. When Tabitha's cheeks puffed up and her face turned as red as a ripe tomato, I added, "Don't shoot the messenger. Blame her parents, not us."

I thought I had gone too far, so I turned back to the cop. He was still speaking. "She hit a tree."

Max wiped his forehead. "Let me get this straight. She was driving, and her car hit a tree?"

Constable Clancy nodded vigorously. "That's right." He gestured expansively to the northwest. "You know that sharp bend on the way to the M1 from here, heading north?" Max nodded. "Instead of turning, her car went pretty much straight ahead, and she hit a big tree."

"We had better check whether she had been drinking," Max said.

The cop nodded. "And maybe she had a heart attack and blacked out, losing control of the car and hitting the tree."

Max tapped his chin. "It's strange that the car went straight ahead and didn't turn."

"Then why are you investigating, Max?" Tabitha asked him. "It's obviously a heart attack.

I've lost count of the number of people I've known who have had heart attacks in cars."

"It's just that she was a very unpopular person in town and she had a lot of enemies," I explained to Tabitha and the others, who were all now standing behind her.

Delilah's jaw dropped open. "Why, what did she do?"

"You know how there's the old bylaw in town that makes coffee illegal?" They all nodded. I pushed on. "The Town Council wanted to bring a motion to overthrow that policy."

Jack interjected. "But I thought that was impossible, given the nature of the law?"

Max nodded slowly. "It would be extremely difficult, but Sheila McFeeler supported the bylaw strongly. She was one of the Town Councillors."

"Why would anyone oppose drinking coffee?" Jack asked. He was clearly perplexed, and rightfully so.

"Because she wanted a traditional town, and she thought coffee being illegal was a point of interest in attracting tourists."

Jack held up both hands to the sky, palms upwards. "Max, what tourist doesn't drink coffee?"

I agreed with him. "I know, it's crazy all right, but she argued violently against it."

Jack patted his son on the shoulder. "All right, Max, you just have to find someone who really loves their coffee, and that will be your murderer."

"But we don't know if she was murdered!" Tabitha shrieked, clearly put out. "She probably simply had a heart attack, for goodness' sake. You all have overactive imaginations!"

Jack ignored her and continued. "Is there a café owner? Maybe someone who has opened a new café?"

"As a matter of fact, there is," I said.

Max turned to me and waved one finger at me. "Goldie, you are absolutely not investigating this. Do you understand me?"

"Sure," I said. "I have no interest in the case, anyway. It's not as if I'm personally involved." It was then I looked up and saw Oleander and Athanasius. Their faces were white and drawn and they were wiggling their eyebrows at me.

Max kissed me on my cheek. "I'm sorry, Goldie, but I have to go. I'll come back as soon as I can."

I clung to his elbow. "You can't leave me," I said in desperation, looking at his relatives.

Max knew exactly what I meant. "I'm sorry, but I have no option," he said. With that, he was gone, shutting the door behind him.

I turned back to his relatives and plastered a fake smile on my face. "Well then, it looks as though we will have to continue our dinner without Max."

Jack and Delilah smiled at me, but Tabitha frowned. I wondered why Jack would marry a woman so thoroughly unpleasant. Maybe, she was blackmailing him—or maybe I did have an overactive imagination, after all. I hurried back to the table and poured myself a glass of bubbly first—to heck with social niceties!

I drank it as fast as I could. Feeling a little better, I filled the other glasses. Athanasius smiled at me. I was relieved to see he had put his teeth back in. "I'll see to the dinner," I said, intending to take a very long time seeing to the dinner. The less time I spent with Max's relatives, the happier I would be.

Oleander jumped to her feet. "I'll help you," she said. Oleander and I both took off to the kitchen. I reached it first and once Oleander had entered, I shut the door firmly behind us, grateful that the old Queenslander was typical of its type and not an open plan house.

I went to toss the salad, but Oleander tugged on my arm. "Goldie, there's something you must know, and it's really, really bad."

I turned around, a salad fork in my hand. "How bad?" I said.

"Very, *very* bad."

My stomach clenched. "What is that?"

"You know how Sheila McFeeler was born here, and then she left town, and then she came back a few months ago?"

I nodded. "I had heard that. What of it?"

"She was a good friend of your uncle's."

"I didn't know," I said, still puzzled.

Oleander shook her head. "No, Goldie, you don't understand."

I raised my eyebrows. "Maybe I would if you explained it."

"Goldie, Sheila McFeeler was a sea witch."

"A sea witch?" I repeated. "Why didn't you tell me? I thought I was the only sea witch in town!"

Oleander hesitated. "Well, I don't know if she was for sure, but she was a good friend of your uncle's…"

I interrupted her. "Surely, all his friends weren't sea witches?"

Oleander waved one hand at me in dismissal. "It's not just that. I think she was a sea witch, because when things didn't go her way, a storm always brewed."

"A coincidence?" I offered.

She shook her head. "I would have mentioned it to you, but it's only become clear in hindsight. I heard that someone accosted her in a café yesterday and argued with her about her trying to prevent coffee from becoming legal. The argument became quite heated, and a violent thunderstorm came up right at that moment. It wasn't an expected storm—I'm subscribed to the email storm alerts, and I didn't get one."

"Do you mean that bad thunderstorm the other day?" I asked her. "The one that appeared with no warning, and there was hail?"

Oleander nodded. "I was only forming suspicions at the time, and I did intend to tell you. But Goldie, don't you see what this means? If Sheila McFeeler was actually murdered, then the murderer might be coming after you too."

I dropped the salad fork into the kitchen sink

and leant back against the sink, grabbing it with both hands. "Oh no! If a witch murders a sea witch, then they get that sea witch's powers. If someone murdered her, then they might be about to murder me too!"

CHAPTER 3

Oleander tapped her chin and looked at the ceiling for a few moments before answering. "The police don't know if it's murder yet. We have to get to Sheila McFeeler's house and search it."

I held up both hands. "Search it? What on earth would we look for?"

"Duh! Witch stuff, of course," Oleander said. "We have to know if she was a sea witch. Goldie, her death might have been an accident, but if she was, in fact, murdered, it might have been a mundane thing, somebody angry with her trying to uphold the anti-coffee law in town. Still, we can't take any chances. If Sheila was a sea witch, then we have to know for sure, because the murderer might come after you next."

Something occurred to me. "Even if she was a sea witch, it could be a coincidence that she was murdered. I mean, her sea witch-ness might have had nothing to do with her murder. It was possibly a mundane reason and that means I'm safe."

Without responding, Oleander pushed past me. She donned some oven mitts, reached into the oven, and with one fluid motion dumped the dinner into the kitchen sink.

"What on earth are you doing?" I screeched. "Have you lost your mind?"

Oleander did not respond but looked under the kitchen cupboard. "Aha! You have some." She emerged with a bottle of kerosene, which she poured into the kitchen sink.

She waved her hand at me. "Stand back!" She threw the kerosene over the dinner and flicked a match on top. The dinner went off with a boom. I grabbed the fire blanket propped against my fridge and threw it over the flames.

Athanasius burst into the room. "What's going on in here?" he asked, his brow furrowed.

"Oleander just set fire to the dinner!"

"We don't have time for that, Goldie,"

Oleander said to me. To Athanasius, she said, "I suspect Sheila McFeeler was a sea witch, so Goldie and I are going to break into her house to see what we can find. You keep Max's relatives occupied, and tell them that we have to go out and buy food. Tell them the dinner is ruined."

"It *is* ruined," I muttered.

"Of course, I will," Athanasius said calmly. I wondered why he took it all in his stride when I was in such a panic.

I stood there, frozen to the spot, my mouth opening and shutting like a goldfish. Oleander grabbed my arm and pulled me into the dining room.

"I'm afraid the dinner is burnt. Goldie and I are going out for takeaway," she announced. "I'll leave you in the capable hands of Athanasius. Athanasius, if Persnickle wakes up, put one of those episodes on for him." She gestured to a pile of *Starsky and Hutch* DVDs by the TV.

"Certainly."

Jack said something, but I didn't hear because I was already half out the door. Oleander must have grabbed my car keys on the way because she pressed them into my hand. She didn't speak again until we were in the car. "Goldie, are you all right?"

"I'm a bit shocked by this sudden turn of events," I admitted.

Oleander made a clicking sound with her tongue. "Honestly, Goldie, get with the program! We have a thin window of opportunity to search Sheila's house before the police arrive."

"What if it's locked?"

She looked over at me. "Can't you drive any faster? And why would her house be locked? Nobody locks houses in the country."

"Just in case they do, do you know how to pick locks?"

"Goldie, if you keep talking about the house being locked, you will manifest it," Oleander said in a lecturing tone. "Oh, turn left here. And drive past her house to see if the police are there, and then keep going. We will have to park away from the house in case Max himself is on the scene. You don't want him to see your car outside the victim's house."

"That's for sure!" I said with feeling.

Sheila McFeeler's house was on the edge of town. I was relieved to see there were no houses around, because people in small country towns know everybody else's business. I drove slowly past the house and then down the road. "Turn left," Oleander said.

"What if I get bogged?" I asked her. "It's not a road, just some kind of weird old track through the mangrove swamp."

"Just go in there, Goldie," Oleander said. "You're being quite difficult today."

I rolled my eyes and drove into the bushes. I called the Indian restaurant and put in our order, before jumping out of the car. Mosquitoes at once attacked me. I slapped them away. Oleander looked down and saw my shoes. "Oh dear. You should have changed into some sensible shoes."

"You're right," I said with dismay. "Anyway, it's too late now."

We hunched over and scurried through the bushes, coming up behind her house. She had a lovely garden of tropical plants in what appeared to me to be a Bali inspired design. "Thank goodness, the police aren't here yet," Oleander said. "Let's try the back door."

Oleander turned the handle, but just as I suspected, it was locked. "It's locked!" she wailed.

"I always lock my doors," I told her.

"But you're from the city and Sheila isn't, or rather wasn't. Let's find an open window."

We walked along the back porch, trying all the windows. They all appeared to be shut. Oleander reached the end window before I did. "This one isn't locked," she said.

The two of us pushed and shoved and could only get the window open a little. "Goldie, see if you can find something in the back yard that will give us leverage."

I tiptoed into the back yard, dismayed that my heels were leaving big pointed holes in the grass, and grabbed a rake. I hurried back as fast as I could.

The rake clearly met with Oleander's approval. She took it from me with a big smile and stuck it between the window and the windowsill, before leveraging it up. Still, the window didn't open all the way. "Goldie, you're much skinnier than I am. You go through first."

"What if there's a toilet on the other side?" I said.

"It's not a bathroom," she countered. "Quick! We mightn't have much time. Once you're through, hurry and open the back door for me."

I edged myself through the window bit by bit

and landed with a thud on the floor. I picked myself up, dusted myself off, and hurried to the back door. It unlocked easily. I let Oleander in. Before she could say anything, I sat on a nearby chair and took off my heels, which I placed outside the back door. Now, I would be able to move around more easily and stealthily.

Oleander tapped me on the shoulder. "Be careful. If she was a sea witch, she would have protection set up around the house. We don't want to stumble into any curses or hexes."

I tiptoed into the living room, but Oleander grabbed my arm. "We don't need to sneak around. We just need to hurry before the police come. She lived alone, so no one is going to hear us."

I felt foolish. "Sure." I walked to the fridge and looked inside. There was nothing much of note, just a half-opened packet of mozzarella and a bottle of wine, and the freezer held several microwaveable dinners. The air conditioner wasn't on, so I lingered in the fridge, letting the cool air wash over me perhaps a little longer than I should have. I still wasn't used to the Queensland humidity.

I heard a shriek and slammed the fridge door.

"In here!" Oleander yelled.

"Where are you?" I called back.

"I told you! I'm in here," she yelled again.

Luckily, Oleander was in the first room I looked in. "It's an altar room," she said, somewhat unnecessarily. Against the far window was a chest of drawers, on top of which was a black altar cloth with three embroidered pentacles placed at intervals across it.

Various crystals and candles adorned the top of the altar. To the side was a glass-fronted cabinet. I crossed to look inside. I reached out to open the door, but Oleander slapped my hand away. "Best not to touch anything," she said, "and when we go home, we should take a cleansing bath, with Epsom salts and salt. Maybe even a pinch of copper sulphate, but at the very least take some rue from your garden and put in the bath. Don't use any soap and either submerge your head or pour water over your head seven times. Air dry, don't towel dry. Take a cup of the bathwater, and after your bath, throw it to the east."

"I know what a cleansing bath is, Oleander," I said wearily. "This means Sheila McFeeler *was* a sea witch, and so the murderer will come after me next." A cold chill ran up my spine. My stomach clenched, and a wave of nausea rolled over me.

Oleander shrugged one shoulder. "Not necessarily. It might be a coincidence, and her murder might not have been at the hands of a witch. After all, she had plenty of mundane enemies. Maybe, one of those did away with her, and you're quite safe." Just as I allowed myself a small glimmer of hope, she added, "But we can't take any chances. Somebody could try to murder you at any time."

"Thanks," I said dryly.

"We have to face facts, Goldie," she said briskly. "Now, let's see if there are any name papers."

"How would that help us?" I asked her. "Besides, you said not to touch anything."

"I'm not a sea witch, so it's probably best if I'm the one to touch any stuff," Oleander said. "I'm thinking that if Sheila had any enemies, she might have been doing spells against them, and maybe she wrote their names on name papers and set them under candles."

"That's a good idea," I said. "Look Oleander, she has another little table over there, and there's a candle on that. It's a black candle, so maybe she was doing a work against an enemy."

Oleander hurried over to the table. "I do believe you're right. That's probably a work *against* someone rather than a work *for* someone, considering it's not on her main altar." She reached out her hand. "Look! There seems to be a lot of copper sulphate and black salt over it, as well as red chilli pepper. Yes, this is definitely a work against someone." She pulled some tweezers out of her pocket and reached for the paper.

"Why are you carrying tweezers in your pocket?" I asked her.

She had no time to respond because we heard a squeal of tyres outside. "The cops!" Oleander said in alarm.

CHAPTER 4

We tiptoed to the front window and peeked around the curtains. There was a uniformed car outside, and as if that wasn't bad enough, Max's car pulled up behind it.

One of the uniformed cops jumped out and headed for the back of the house.

"Let's make a sprint for it now!" Oleander said.

I grabbed her arm. "No! He'll see us for sure. We have to hide in the house."

We desperately looked around the house. Sadly, there was no tablecloth over the dining room table. It had a pretty runner across its length, on top of which were glass-encased candles.

"Could we hide behind the sofa?" Oleander asked, followed by, "Forget that!"

"We'll have to hide in the kitchen cupboards!" I said. "Quick!" I grabbed Oleander by the elbow and dragged her over to the kitchen cupboards. I certainly hoped they weren't crammed full of stuff. I was in luck. One of the cupboards had no shelves, no doubt to make room for the tall food processor against one wall. "I'll fit in there!" I said.

"What about me?" Oleander squeaked.

I opened the corner cupboard. "Oh, thank goodness, there's nothing in there except recyclable plastic bags."

Oleander bent down to look, and I pushed her inside.

"I'm stuck!" she squeaked.

"Try harder," I said. I put my hands on her bottom and pushed for all I was worth. With a muffled groan, followed by several muffled, very rude words, Oleander's bottom disappeared from view, as did her legs. I had trouble shutting the door, but I finally managed. I returned to the cupboard I had selected and climbed inside, before pulling the door shut behind me.

I fought back the panic. I didn't like being in enclosed spaces but realised it was a choice between two evils. What would I rather do, hide in an enclosed space or have Max find me? I decided on the former. There really was no choice.

I certainly hoped the cops wouldn't look in the kitchen cupboards, but since I figured they didn't know yet if Sheila McFeeler was murdered, I supposed they were having a cursory look. Still, they seemed to be taking forever. I hugged my knees and tried to breathe slowly. I breathed in for three, held my breath for four, and let my breath out for five. That only served to make me feel as though I couldn't get enough air. It was hot in the cupboard.

I could hear their voices, but I couldn't make out what they were saying. Mercifully, after what seemed like an age, I heard them making their way towards the front door. I decided to count to two hundred and then climb out stealthily. I had watched too many horror movies where people left their hiding places too soon.

I lost interest after counting to fifty and opened the cupboard door. No one was in sight. I took a deep breath of fresh air, wiped the sweat from my forehead, and hurried over to the window to peek out. Sure enough, Max and two uniformed officers were talking on the front porch.

I ran back on my bare feet to the kitchen cupboard and opened it. I pulled on Oleander's legs until she emerged from the cupboard. "Oleander, are you all right? Your face is bright red."

"I was on my head the whole time," she said in a small voice. "I was stuck!"

"Well, there's no time for complaining now," I whispered. "They're on the porch. Now is the time to run. Or maybe they're going to come back inside. Perhaps we should hide in the cupboards again for a while longer."

"No, I'm not hiding in that cupboard again!" Oleander hissed. "Goldie, let's hightail it out of here!"

Before I could protest, she took my wrist in a vice-like grip and dragged me to the back door.

A big ginger cat blocked our way.

"Oh no! Sheila had a kitty. Who will look after the kitty now?" I asked.

Oleander frowned. "As far as I know, Sheila didn't have any relatives. Maybe, they will put the cat in the pound."

The cat looked alarmed. I grabbed the cat, who did his best to scratch me. Strangely enough, he purred loudly while trying to get a paw free.

"This cat is not going to any pound!" I said. "We'll have to take him with us."

"He must have been Sheila's familiar! Sea witches have familiars. What are we going to do?"

There was a noise outside the front door. "Hurry, Goldie, now! We have to leave!"

I ran after Oleander to the back door. Oleander shut it quietly behind us and then we sprinted for the mangrove swamp at the back of the house.

"Ouch! Ouch, ouch!" I said, followed by a few rather rude words.

"What's wrong?" Oleander whispered.

"The cat scratched me," I began, but the cat scratched me again and I dropped him by reflex.

Oleander dive-bombed on the cat and grabbed him around his middle. He proceeded to scratch her.

"Poor thing, he's scared," I said, followed by, "Oh! I think you need some Band-Aids."

Oleander handed the cat to me. I took him gingerly. The adrenaline was beginning to wear off, and I remembered my feet were bare. "I left my shoes by the back door," I said.

Oleander gasped. "That's terrible!"

"No, it's not too bad," I said. "They weren't Jimmy Choos."

Oleander rubbed her forehead. "No, I meant the police will see the heels. I very much doubt Sheila McFeeler ever wore heels as high as that."

"Don't worry about it," I said. "They're men! They won't know what sort of heels she wore. I bet they won't even notice them. I'll sneak back later and get them." We made our way to the car. I breathed a sigh of relief when it didn't get bogged, and I drove in the other direction as fast as I could.

When I got to the Indian restaurant, I left Oleander in the car with the cat, and left the engine running with the air conditioning on. The lady at the restaurant told me our order would be another two minutes, but just as she said it, someone brought our food out of the kitchen. I paid and hurried back to the car.

"That was a stroke of brilliant timing," I told Oleander. "Our order came out of the kitchen just as I got there. I told them we've been sitting outside in the car this whole time. That way, if the police happen to ask her, she'll tell them we waited in the car. She won't think twice, and the police won't think to ask her how she knew."

Oleander appeared to be in complete admiration. "You're so clever, Goldie!"

"I know," I said smugly. "Before we go home, I'll have to buy a litter box and cat food."

Oleander was eyeing the cat warily. He certainly didn't seem to have a good temperament, or maybe he was simply frightened. "Oh good, sounds like a plan."

When we got to the house, I said, "Won't they wonder why I have bare feet? And won't Max wonder why I suddenly have a strange cat?"

"Just tell Max he's a stray," Oleander said. "Anyway, we have a bigger problem than that."

"You mean apart from Max finding out what we did?"

"Yes, have you noticed the cat's colour?"

"Ginger?" As soon as I saw it, it dawned on me. "Oh no! Orange! Persnickle is going to hate him."

"We can't let them meet," Oleander said. "Okay, this is what we'll do. I'll go inside and go into your bedroom, and I'll pass shoes out the window to you. You hand me the cat, the cat food, and the litter box. Actually, you might need to make two trips—hand me the cat first. And hurry before Max gets back here."

I thought the plan wouldn't work, but to my surprise, it all went smoothly.

When the cat was safely inside, I walked into the house. "Sorry about burning the dinner," I said.

Tabitha glared at me, but Jack and Delilah smiled widely. "Think nothing of it," Jack said. "It was very kind of you to go and buy some. May I make a contribution?"

"Thanks for your kind offer, but I absolutely insist," I said. "It was entirely my fault."

"Actually, it was my fault," Oleander interjected. "I was the one who burnt the dinner."

"You were a long time!" Tabitha snapped.

"Yes, I thought there was something wrong with the air-conditioning in the car, so I was checking it out before I came in," I lied.

"I didn't know you knew about the mechanics of cars," Jack said.

I frowned. "I don't. That's why I took so long."

Jack looked confused but didn't respond.

Oleander beckoned to Athanasius. "Athanasius, I need your help in the kitchen."

"I wonder if Max will be back at any minute?" Delilah said to nobody in particular.

"No, he'll be a while," I began, but then

caught myself. "These police matters usually take a long time, but I've saved some food for him."

We ate our Indian food in peace, which was short-lived, as I soon heard a cat meow.

"What's that noise?" Tabitha asked.

I clutched my stomach and swallowed my mouthful of wine the wrong way. "What noise?" I asked when I recovered.

"Maybe you heard a bunyip," Athanasius said. "I didn't hear anything. They say if you hear a bunyip that you're going to die that very night."

"What nonsense!" Tabitha's cheeks swelled up. "I don't believe in those mythical creatures."

The cat meowed again.

Persnickle jumped to his feet and ran around the room in circles. "It's those stray cats again," I said. "Some of them have been hanging around outside." I hurried to the TV and put on another episode of *Starsky and Hutch*. Persnickle snuggled into his wombat bed but kept looking around the room. I certainly hoped he wasn't going to give the game away.

Athanasius obviously thought so too, because he said, "Let's put on some music. There's nothing like music with a dinner party, is there?" He pulled out his phone and flipped through it.

The sounds of heavy metal music ripped through the air.

Tabitha opened her mouth to protest, but Oleander leant over to her. "Don't complain, whatever you do. He's very attached to his music, and he gets upset when people complain about it. The doctor says it's bad for his heart."

To my surprise, Tabitha shut her mouth. The rest of the main meal passed without incident. I hadn't heard the cat meow again, possibly because of Athanasius's music, but I hoped he had settled down.

I went into the kitchen to fetch dessert, which, thankfully, Oleander hadn't burnt. Oleander soon burst through the kitchen door. "I've just been into your bedroom and the cat is fast asleep on your pillow," she said. "I'll take him back to the retirement home with me."

"Are you allowed to have pets?" I asked her.

She looked offended. "Goldie, it's a retirement home, not a prison."

"But they don't allow pets in some apartments at the Gold Coast," I said. "And if you're allowed to have pets, why haven't you had one before now?"

"Athanasius isn't allowed to have a pet because

he's in the main complex. I'm allowed to have a pet. It's just that I haven't until now because I used to do a lot of travelling. I'll keep him until we find a good home for him."

"What if Max finds out Sheila McFeeler had a cat?" I asked her.

"Even if he does, it won't matter. One ginger cat looks pretty much the same as another to most people," Oleander pointed out.

I waved my finger at her. "You're forgetting! Cats in this country have to be microchipped by law. If Max takes the cat to the vet and the vet runs a microchip scanner over him, he'll know that Sheila McFeeler is the owner."

Oleander smiled widely. "Why would Max take somebody else's cat to the vet to have him scanned? No, I think everything will be fine. Leave it to me. You'll see."

I sure didn't share her confidence.

Max returned seconds after I walked back into the dining room. He walked through the door, waving a pair of heels. "Do these look familiar, Goldie?" he said by way of greeting.

I hoped a guilty look had not flashed across my face. "Whose are those?" I asked with forced nonchalance. "They're not Jimmy Choos."

"We found them at Sheila McFeeler's house."

Athanasius spoke up. "Why did you remove Sheila's shoes from her house? Will they be used in evidence?"

"How would they possibly be used in evidence?" Oleander asked him. To Max, she said, "Was Sheila murdered with a stiletto?"

Max frowned deeply. I suspected he knew I had been at the house. "So, were you here all night all evening, Goldie? You didn't leave the house?"

I looked at Oleander. "Actually, I burnt the dinner, so we had to go to the Indian restaurant to get takeaway," she said. "We waited at the restaurant the whole time. Why do you ask?"

Max narrowed his eyes and looked directly at me. "No reason," he said.

I decided to change the subject. "So, what happened to Sheila McFeeler? Do you think it was a heart attack?"

I was certainly hoping it had been an accident and not a murder. Of course, it didn't make any difference to Sheila McFeeler, who had now crossed over to the other side, but it would certainly make a difference to me if somebody tried to come and murder me. I held my breath, waiting for Max's answer.

"It was definitely murder," he said.

"But can you be sure?" Athanasius asked him. "Surely, there hasn't been time for a post-mortem?"

Max shook his head. "There's no need for a post-mortem. Her brake lines were cut."

And just when I thought things couldn't get any worse, the ginger cat strolled into the room.

CHAPTER 5

Athanasius at once turned off his music. I looked at Persnickle, wondering if I should lunge at him, but to my enormous relief, he had fallen asleep.

Max put his hands on his hips. "Is that Sheila McFeeler's cat?"

I plastered an innocent look on my face. "What? She had a cat?"

Oleander hurried to the rescue. "You're kidding! Do you really think it's her cat? What an amazing coincidence. When Goldie and I were waiting in the car outside the Indian restaurant, that cat walked right past us. I grabbed him and put him in the car, and we brought him home."

Max obviously didn't believe a word of it.

"Why would you bring home a cat?" he said through gritted teeth.

Oleander tut-tutted. "Well, it isn't safe for a cat to be out on the street, is it? Not for the cat and not for the native animals. I didn't want to take him to the pound, so we brought him back. I was going to take him to the retirement home later and put a lost and found notice on the Facebook community page."

"I thought you said it was a stray," Tabitha snapped.

"No, I said, there are strays around," Oleander corrected her. "This cat is obviously well cared for."

The cat walked over to Max and rubbed his head on his leg. Max picked up the cat and held him to his chest. The cat purred loudly, and Max scratched him under the chin. "Nice kitty," he said. "I'll take the cat to the vet and have him scanned to see who the owner is."

"I thought you said cops would never do that," Oleander said to me.

"You were the one who said it, Oleander." To Max, I said, "And what if he is Sheila McFeeler's cat? You don't want the poor cat to end up in a pound, do you?"

"If he is her cat, he can stay with me, and we'll see if any relatives come forward to claim him." Max looked at the cat fondly. "I've always wanted a cat."

"So, you want to keep him?" I was incredulous.

Max stroked the cat's head. The cat climbed onto his shoulder and wrapped his paws around Max's neck.

I was rather shocked that the cat did not attempt to scratch Max. I was also surprised that Max would take home an orange cat. Persnickle hated the colour orange, and he would hate an orange cat. Sure, it would be a good home for the cat, but didn't Max see a future between us? My stomach sank. Or maybe Max hadn't put two and two together. In that case, Persnickle would have to learn to like the cat somehow. Maybe I could train him with carrots—*lots* of carrots.

Max was still speaking. "Can the cat stay here until after dinner, Goldie?"

I was relieved. "Sure! So, you're not rushing off now?"

Max shook his head. "I'm starving, and it's been a long day."

Oleander held out her hands. "I'll put the cat

back in the room in case Persnickle sees him, and then you can take him after dinner."

"Persnickle doesn't like cats?" Max asked in surprise. "He was fine with the pademelon."

"The pademelon wasn't orange."

Max looked surprised, and then his mouth formed a perfect O. "I hadn't thought of that."

He continued to frown until Oleander took the cat into my room. When she returned, she said, "Max, you sit down, and I'll fetch your dinner. We saved some for you. When she returned, she put the plate under Max's nose.

He looked at it before asking, "I didn't know we were having curry for dinner?"

"Oleander burnt the dinner, which is why we had to go to the Indian restaurant. We just explained that."

Max rubbed his forehead. "Okay, don't tell me any more. It's all too much for me."

I poured him a glass of champagne. "This will make everything seem better." We all sat around the table and chatted while Max ate his dinner.

"So, you said somebody cut her brake lines?" Tabitha asked. "Do they really do that? I thought it was only in movies."

"They obviously do it, because they did it," Max said. I could tell he was still a little tense.

"But there are no cliffs around here," I continued. "On TV, people always cut brake lines on cars of people who are about to drive down a mountain or something like that."

"Sheila McFeeler went to Brisbane frequently, and that's a fast road. When she went to slow down, she wouldn't have been able to brake at that sharp bend, and that's precisely how she was killed."

"Oh, I see." I thought some more and then said, "I wonder who would want her dead?"

"Plenty of people, obviously," Athanasius said, "what with her supporting the anti-coffee law. And she was about to open that new tearoom."

Max set down his fork with a thud and looked up. "She was? What café?"

Athanasius pushed on. "It wasn't a café as such. It was a tearoom—you know, like an English tearoom. It would only serve tea and not coffee."

"But English tearooms serve coffee too," I said to Athanasius.

He shrugged. "That's why I thought her whole support for the anti-coffee law was totally self interest. This is becoming more and more a tourist area and I'm sure tourists would prefer to go to a specialist tearoom that serves all sorts of different teas, rather than go to a coffee shop that doesn't serve coffee."

Max stroked his chin. He had a five o'clock shadow, and his eyes look tired. My heart went out to him. "Tell me all you know, Athanasius."

"I don't know much more than that," Athanasius said. "It's just that word on the street was that Sheila had already taken out the lease of the building."

"Why didn't you tell me?" Oleander asked him.

"I only found out this morning," Athanasius said. "I was walking through town and saw someone removing the For Lease sign on the building. I asked the man who was doing it, and he told me Sheila McFeeler was setting up an English tearoom with all different varieties of tea as well as specialty cakes."

"Thanks, Athanasius. You've been very helpful." Max ate the rest of his dinner, and silence fell over the room.

I allowed myself a small measure of relief. Perhaps the murderer was one of the people who owned one of the cafés in town. Maybe there was another reason for disposing of Sheila.

I tried to think of motives for murder and came up with love, money, wrong-place-wrong-time, and revenge. I had even seen a movie where somebody was murdered because the captions had been mixed up on a photo in the local paper, and it was a case of mistaken identity. I supposed there were other motives of murder, but I couldn't think of any right now.

Did Sheila McFeeler have a boyfriend? I had no idea, but I was certainly going to look into it. Maybe, she was having an affair, and her lover's jealous wife had murdered her. Maybe, it was someone who had a commercial interest in coffee. Athanasius was right —East Bucklebury had always been a tourist attraction, and more and more tourists were attracted to the area all the time. The Town Council was keen on promoting it as a tourist area, and Sheila McFeeler's support of the anti-coffee law would certainly work against tourism in the area.

Perhaps the murderer was somebody who had a vested interest in local tourism. I rubbed my forehead. My head was beginning to spin. One thing was clear—Sheila had been a sea witch, and she could well have been murdered for that reason.

In previous murders, I had taken Persnickle to question the victims, but Sheila could not have possibly witnessed her own murder, because she wasn't there when the murderer had cut her brake lines.

I looked up and saw Max staring at me. "Oh, would you like dessert?"

"That would be lovely, thanks."

I took his empty curry plate to the kitchen, stuck it in the dishwasher, and piled some cheesecake and ice cream into a bowl. When I walked back into the dining room, I saw Jack, Delilah, and Tabitha all standing by the door. "We have to be on our way," Jack said. "Thank you for dinner, Goldie, it was lovely."

"The curry at least was edible," Tabitha said through narrowed eyes.

"Do you have to leave too, Delilah?" I asked her.

She nodded. "Yes, because Jack is taking me back to my hotel room."

"We are *both* going to take you back to your hotel room," Tabitha snapped.

Delilah looked quite put out. "Yes, I meant

that I don't have a car, so somebody will have to take me, and you and Jack have a car each."

"Why did you bring two cars instead of one?" I asked Jack. It hadn't occurred to me before, but it did seem awfully strange that a couple would arrive in two separate cars. As soon as I asked, I regretted the question because Tabitha looked daggers at me.

Jack laughed. "It *is* strange, I know, but Tabitha doesn't like my driving. She always insists on taking her own car everywhere."

With a nod, Tabitha disappeared through the door, followed by Jack and Delilah.

I looked out the door and waved. When they had driven away, I returned to the table and sat with the others. "Max, why aren't they staying with you?" I asked him.

Max laughed for the first time that night. "You've met them, haven't you! I mean, I get along with my father and my mother but not with Tabitha."

"Why didn't you just have Delilah stay with you then?"

"Because Tabitha would have objected," Max said. "I really don't know what my father sees in that woman. She's entirely obnoxious." He rubbed his eyes. "Goldie, if you don't mind, I'll go home now. This is going to be a murder investigation, so I've got a lot of paperwork to do."

"Sure," I said. Max stood up and pulled me into a long kiss. When he released me, Oleander and Athanasius were both chuckling like teenagers. I shot them a dirty look.

"No investigating, you three," Max said sternly, before he disappeared through my front door.

"Of course not!" I called after him.

"We wouldn't dream of it," said Oleander.

"Too right!" Athanasius agreed.

I shut the front door and locked it, and then looked through the window to make sure Max wasn't eavesdropping.

"He forgot the cat," I said. "And thankfully, my shoes."

"Which means he'll be back for the cat," Oleander said. "So, let's keep our voices down. Now, how do we begin this investigation?"

"Oleander told me Sheila McFeeler was indeed a sea witch," Athanasius said, his expression grim. "Goldie, that means the murderer will come after you next. You'll have to lock all your doors and windows. Is it even safe for you to stay here?"

Oleander tapped him on the shoulder. "Goldie's gone quite white. You're scaring her!"

"Better scared and alive than not scared and dead," Athanasius said primly. "I think we should move in with Goldie and arm ourselves."

I thought Oleander would say that was a silly idea, but she readily agreed. "I think we should too, but what about room service?" she asked Athanasius.

"Room service?" I echoed.

"We often help out at the retirement home." A strange look passed over her face.

"The others can do it," he said.

Oleander nodded. "Goldie, I know that means you won't get any alone time with Max until this matter is solved but safety first and all that."

"Sure," I said.

"You could use your sea witch powers against any witch who comes to kill you, but obviously they took Sheila by surprise. As soon as you get into your car, test your brakes," Oleander said.

Athanasius nodded. "And what are some other ways the murderer could kill Goldie? Apart from cutting her brake lines, I mean. You have to think ahead."

"Maybe they will run over you when you're crossing the road," Oleander said. "You have to be extra careful crossing roads. Maybe don't cross any roads at all—park on the side of the road and stay on that side when you're in town."

Athanasius tapped his chin. "There's always shooting and stabbing and poisoning. Goldie, don't eat anything from an open jar."

I clutched my head as the two of them thought of all the ways somebody could murder me. Finally, I held up one hand, palm outwards. "Could you guys stop! I'm really scared now. Besides, we have to consider the possibility that a witch didn't murder her."

Athanasius looked quite put out. "Whatever do you mean, Goldie?"

"I mean, sure she was a sea witch and so any evil witch would want to murder her to get her powers, but she also supported the old anti-coffee bylaw, and that made her plenty of enemies. On the other hand, maybe it was a mundane murder and I'm completely safe."

"You're right," Oleander said, "but it's like Athanasius said, we can't take any chances. The first thing to do is to take Persnickle to the scene of her death, so you can question her ghost."

"Wouldn't the ghost go back to her own house?" I asked.

Oleander held out her glass for more bubbly. I filled it. She sipped some and then said, "Yes, but the police could be at her house. At least the place she died was a public place and the police shouldn't still be there."

"Sheila wouldn't know who killed her. She obviously wasn't there when her brake lines were cut, so that's not much help," I said.

Athanasius disagreed. "She will know who her enemies were. You could also ask her if she knew she was in any danger from another witch in town."

Something occurred to me. I waved my finger at them both. "You know, you're right! If somebody murdered her because she was a sea witch, then that somebody must be new to town. We could find out who's just moved to town."

I thought my idea was a good one, but I was soon disavowed of that notion. Oleander shook her head. "It could be a tourist, Goldie. A tourist could have found out she was sea witch after being in town for just a few days. They could have cut her brake lines, and then left town."

I groaned. "And that makes our job harder."

My bedroom door opened again, and the cat stalked out. "How does he do that?" I asked.

No one had a chance to respond, because Persnickle woke up. His little wombat eyes widened at the sight of the orange cat. He made a horrible grunting sound and then charged at the cat. "Stop!" I shrieked. "Somebody, help!"

Persnickle charged onwards. When Persnickle was only inches away from the cat, the cat made the most horrible sound I had ever heard, and his hair stood on end. So did mine.

The cat reached out one paw and struck at Persnickle. Persnickle did a sliding stop on his bottom, his front legs stretched out. He only managed to change course at the last moment. He then turned around and sprinted for the sofa and wasted no time hiding under it. The trouble was, he was taller than the underneath of the sofa, so the sofa lifted on both ends and wobbled precariously. I ran to the kitchen to get carrots to soothe him, while Oleander grabbed the cat.

Just then, there was a knock on the door. I threw carrots under the sofa and hurried to open the door. Tabitha was standing there. "I forgot my handbag," she snapped.

To my horror, she was wearing bright orange pyjamas.

The fact was not lost on Persnickle. The cat forgotten, he charged from under the sofa and grabbed one of Tabitha's pyjama bottom legs. Tabitha screamed and tried to pull back. Her pyjama bottoms came off in Persnickle's mouth. He tore at them with his front paws and ripped them to shreds.

I looked up to see Tabitha running down my front path in her huge, pink, floral underwear, screaming obscenities at the top of her lungs.

CHAPTER 6

When I awoke the next morning, I was relieved I was still alive. I had tossed and turned all night and had jumped at every noise. Max had texted me just after midnight to ask if I could keep the cat until the following day. I had no idea what I had texted back, as I was only half awake.

I staggered into the kitchen and pulled the cover off the coffee machine. Max agreed that we couldn't trust his relatives enough to let them know I had an illegal coffee machine in the house. I figured he was referring to Tabitha.

I could hear dreadful snoring and thought it was Persnickle until I realised it was Athanasius. As I walked out with my coffee, Oleander appeared and Persnickle awoke. I gave Persnickle a carrot and handed Oleander a steaming mug of coffee.

"The night passed uneventfully enough," she said. "I expect the murderer won't strike so soon, realising that you'll be on your guard."

"At least we can rule out long-term town residents," I said. "I mean, a long-term town resident might have murdered Sheila, but I doubt a long-term town resident was a witch who was after Sheila's powers."

"How was the cat?" Oleander asked me.

"He was good. I thought he might purr loudly and wake me up at night or sleep on my feet, but he slept at the end of the bed. I fed him and made sure the door was firmly shut before I came in here to make coffee. I've hardly had a wink of sleep, and I feel dreadful." I drained my coffee and at once made another cup.

"Look, it's early," Oleander said. "Why don't we take Persnickle down to the crime scene and you can speak to the ghost?"

"I hope her ghost *is* at the crime scene." I scratched my head. "What if she's back at her house?"

"Then we go to her house," Oleander said

with a wave of her hand. "It's not as if the house is a crime scene. The police won't have any interest in it whatsoever. They searched it yesterday, and that will be the end of it."

I drew one hand over my forehead. "I do hope you're right. I really don't want Max to catch me."

"Max to catch you doing what?" said the man in question as he walked through the kitchen door.

I gasped and thought quickly. "I meant your relatives catch me with a coffee machine," I lied, considering it wasn't good to lie to the man I loved, but then again, I'm sure he didn't think witches existed. Max would be in for an awful shock if he ever found out I was a witch. I sighed long and hard. Of course I would have to tell him at some point, not just yet.

Max turned his attention to Oleander. "You're here early, and why is Athanasius asleep on the sofa?"

"They stayed here all night," I said. "They wanted to protect me."

Max seemed confused. "Protect you from what?"

"Well, there was a murder, wasn't there!" Oleander said. "Goldie is a woman living on her own, and we were worried about leaving her here.

After all, you don't know who the murderer is and he or she could be a serial killer."

A wearied look crossed Max's face. "Serial killers murder more than one person."

Oleander shrugged. "They have to start somewhere! And if he murders Goldie, then he is well on his way to being a serial killer."

I ignored her and simply asked, "Coffee?"

"Yes, please," Max said with feeling. "Make it a double shot. How is my new cat?" Before I could respond, he added, "I'm going to take him to the vet to have his microchip scanned this morning."

"If he was Sheila McFeeler's cat, are you going to keep him?" Oleander asked him.

"I'd like to." Max shot me a look. "Only, I'm concerned about Persnickle. What if Persnickle attacks him?"

Oleander and I laughed, much to Max's confusion. "Persnickle already tried to attack him last night," I told him. "It was the cat who attacked Persnickle. He's afraid of the cat now."

My mirth was short-lived when I remembered the incident with Tabitha. "Oh Max, your stepmother forgot her handbag. Could you take it back to her? She turned up here in her bright orange pyjamas looking for it." Max gasped. I pushed on. "And Persnickle ripped them off her."

I thought Max would be angry, but he chuckled. "That must have been a sight."

"One that will haunt me to my dying days," Oleander said with a grimace.

I was concerned. "Max, you don't think she will complain to the police that I have a dangerous animal, do you?"

Max laughed. "I *am* the police. Don't worry, my father can handle her."

"Max, if you don't mind me asking, why did your father marry Tabitha? They seem, um, quite different."

Max chuckled again. "Tabitha isn't a nice person. You don't need to tiptoe around that with me. I have no idea why my father married her either. He and my mother are still good friends, and I was always hoping they would get back together, but he married Tabitha and that put paid to that idea."

I shrugged. "Oh well, opposites attract, I'm sure.

"There's a cat carry basket in my bedroom. We went to the pet shop and bought one when the cat turned up yesterday," I told Max. I didn't want to meet his eyes, so I busied myself making another coffee. Luckily, Athanasius walked in and gave Max a blow-by-blow description of Persnickle ripping the pyjama bottoms off Tabitha.

Soon we were all laughing, although I was still a little worried. If a witch had murdered Sheila McFeeler, then I was next on the list. As far as I knew, I was the only other sea witch left in town, but then again, I really wouldn't know. I had not known Sheila was one. There could be more, for all I knew.

Max set down his coffee cup. "I'll take the cat to the vet for microchip scanning, and if he was Sheila's cat, then I'll take him to my house. I'll try to work from home today, and I'll have my parents and Tabitha over to my house. I can spend time with the cat."

"If he was Sheila's cat, then at least the vet will have his name on record," Oleander said.

"That's a good idea. I hadn't thought of that," Max said over his shoulder as he went to fetch the cat.

We all smiled and waved until Max was out of sight before hurrying back inside. This time, I made sure I put on my sensible shoes. I fetched

Persnickle's leash, and we all piled into my car. I drove out towards the scene of Sheila McFeeler's accident, making sure I tested my brakes several times.

"Have you tested your brakes yet, Goldie?" Athanasius asked me.

"She's been testing them all the time, and that's why the car has been jerking," Oleander told him.

"I just thought Goldie's driving was getting worse," Athanasius said. "Would you like me to drive, Goldie?"

I gasped. "No way in… I mean, no thanks." I changed the subject. "Wow, you can get up some speed on this road, that's for sure." As we approached the sharp turn, I said, "Poor Sheila didn't have a hope! You need to slow down a long way before this bend or you'll never make it."

Oleander agreed. "It's been the scene of quite a few accidents. With her brakes cut, she didn't have much of a hope for sure."

I pulled off the road. Luckily, the tow truck had squashed the vegetation, so I was able to get well off the road, which was just as well, as cars kept speeding past me. I got Persnickle out of the car and took him over to a large white gum tree which had marks on it and was surrounded by yellow and black police tape. "This is obviously where the poor woman's car landed," Oleander said. "They didn't waste any time towing her car away."

"No doubt they had to take it to the police lab," I said. "Sheila McFeeler, are you here?"

I expected it would take a long time for her to materialise, so I was shocked when the ghost materialised at once. "You're a sea witch!" she said by way of greeting.

"Yes, I'm Goldie Bloom," I said. "This is my familiar, Persnickle, and these are my good friends, Oleander and Athanasius. They can't see you or hear you—they're not sea witches."

"Is Sheila McFeeler's ghost here now?" Athanasius asked.

Oleander rolled her eyes. "Of course, she is! Goldie wasn't talking to herself."

The ghost looked Oleander and Athanasius up and down. "Yes, I can see that. Is Lucifer all right?"

"Lucifer?" I echoed. Oleander and Athanasius gasped. "Um, I don't know. Did something happen to him? Do you think you're going to hell?"

The ghost seemed exasperated. "My cat!" she snapped.

"Your cat is called Lucifer?"

"Lucifer?" Oleander and Athanasius echoed in unison.

I nodded. "Yes, your cat, um, Lucifer, stayed at my house last night, and my friend Max has taken him to the vet to be scanned. You see, Max doesn't know I'm a sea witch, and so we couldn't tell him that the cat was yours."

"He won't take him to the pound, will he?" the ghost asked in alarm.

I shook my head. "No way! Max wants to keep him. That is, unless you had someone else in mind?"

"Oh, you mean Detective Max Grayson?"

I nodded.

The ghost looked pleased. "I'd love it if he would keep him."

"And now to the matter of your murder," I said. "Max said your brake lines were cut."

"Yes, I figured that out for myself," the ghost said, somewhat snarkily.

"Do you have any idea who could have done it?"

"You're worried it was a witch, aren't you." She said it as a statement, not a question.

I had to admit that I was. "And if it was a witch, then I'm next in line," I told her. "Did you know I was a sea witch before you saw me here just then?"

She shook her head. "And before you ask, no, I don't know any other sea witches in town. We're not common, you know."

"Then if it wasn't a witch murdering you to get your powers, you must have been murdered for a mundane reason," I said, "like for your support of the anti-coffee law in town."

Athanasius stepped forward and addressed the general area in front of me. "Do you have any suspects?"

The ghost shook her head. "No, I can't really think of any. I'm still trying to get over the shock of being dead. Walsh has just bought that large café in town and had it renovated. My tearoom was going to be in direct opposition to him, and he was the Town Councillor who was the most vocal about the anti-coffee bylaw being overturned. He's the one who springs to mind."

I turned around and repeated what she said to Oleander and Athanasius, before turning back to the ghost. "And do you have any other clues?" I asked her. "I mean, were you wealthy? Who stands to inherit?"

The ghost chuckled. "I don't think I have enough money for anyone to kill me over. I don't have any living relatives apart from my son, and I left everything to him. He's currently in Dubai. He's quite a wealthy businessman, so he wouldn't have sent someone to kill me to get my money."

I scratched my head. "Could you give us his name, and we'll check into it just to be on the safe side?"

She shrugged. "You're definitely on the wrong track with him, but his name is Tristan Smith."

I looked over my shoulder at Oleander. "Can you write down Tristan Smith, the heir? Sheila says he's wealthy and in Dubai at the moment, but we should check him out simply to exclude him."

Oleander tapped away in her phone notes and nodded slowly. "So the only main suspect is Walsh?"

Sheila nodded. "I can't think of any motives, but the only thing I can think of would be my support of the anti-coffee law. It would have to be someone who thought coffee would help tourism in this town. Why don't you look into whoever stands to make a lot of money out of tourism?"

"That's a good idea," I said. "You've been very helpful." I turned back to her to say something else, but she had vanished.

Just then, a car pulled up behind mine. To my dismay, it was Max's.

He marched over to me and put his hands on his hips. "What are you doing here, Goldie?" he demanded in a steely tone.

CHAPTER 7

"I asked Goldie to drive me to Brisbane," Athanasius said. "I wanted to borrow her car, but she refused and said she would drive me."

"It's no wonder, the way you drive!" Oleander said.

Max was having none of it. He continued to stare at me. "So! You're snooping already, Goldie."

"What do you mean?" I said, hoping my acting skills had improved since the last murder. "I was driving Athanasius to Brisbane and Persnickle needed a bathroom break."

Right on cue, Persnickle grunted.

"So, Persnickle just happened to need a bathroom break right at the scene of the accident?"

"Oh, is this where it happened?" Oleander asked.

Max gestured to the police tape. "Obviously!"

"I had no idea."

"And why were you driving to Brisbane?" Max asked me. "Shouldn't you be at your office?"

"It's only eight, and I don't open until nine."

"If you're on your way to Brisbane, you won't be back until around ten," Max said.

I did my best to giggle and look vacant. "You know me, I'm always so mathematically challenged."

"Why were you going to Brisbane?" Max asked again.

"I asked Goldie to drive me there." Athanasius nodded as he spoke.

Max rolled his eyes. "I know that, but *why* did you want to go?"

"I wanted to see what was on at the Brisbane Art Gallery. I heard there was a new exhibition."

"And what exhibition was that?"

"I don't know, and that's why I asked Goldie to drive me."

Max looked decidedly put out. "Goldie, I

know what you're up to. Please don't investigate. Somebody cut Sheila McFeeler's brake lines, and if they know you're investigating, you might be in danger."

"All right then. Max, are you on your way to Brisbane?" I asked him.

"No, I was looking for you and I suspected you'd be here," he said, narrowing his eyes even further so that they were mere slits. "I wondered if I could have your key, so I could fetch the cat and take him home to my place."

"Sure." I pulled the car keys out of my pocket and took off one of the keys. "This is a spare key."

I handed it to him, and our fingers brushed. Electric jolts shot through my body at the contact. I looked at Max, wondering if he had felt it too.

He simply nodded. "I'll leave the key on the table and lock the door behind me. Don't forget, you have dinner tonight with my parents and my stepmother."

I groaned. "I *had* forgotten. I hope your stepmother still isn't angry with me."

"She probably is, but don't worry about it," Max said. "Look, I have to go now. I'll see you at the restaurant tonight, Goldie." With that, he marched over to his police vehicle and sped off.

"Gosh, our timing was bad," I lamented. "Now he knows I'm investigating or *snooping around*, as he puts it. We might as well take Persnickle home and then go back to the office."

"Shouldn't we go to Brisbane to maintain our cover?" Athanasius asked.

I shrugged. "What's the point? Max knew we were lying. And besides, I have to make a living."

"You go to work, and Athanasius and I can investigate Walsh," Oleander said.

Athanasius raised one bushy eyebrow. "I've always wondered if that was his first or his last name."

Oleander shrugged. "I think he only has one name, you know, like Adele, Madonna, or Oprah."

"I see," Athanasius said, although it was clear that he didn't.

"Come on, let's get into the car," I said. As we were driving away, I added, "Is Walsh new in town?"

"No, he's been around for years," Oleander told me. "But he's only just recently opened a café."

"It seems rather a silly thing to do to open a

café in a town that doesn't sell coffee," I pointed out.

Oleander disagreed. "It would seem so on the surface, but he bought the café for a song for that very reason and then thought he could get the old anti-coffee bylaw overturned. Sheila McFeeler was the only one standing in the way of him making money."

I thought it over for a moment before speaking. "I don't know. Even if it was very successful, it *is* East Bucklebury. After all, he's not going to make millions. Is it worth murdering somebody over?"

"I'm sure people have been murdered over less."

"You could be right, Oleander," I said. "I need more coffee after running into Max. When I take Persnickle home, let's all have some coffee before we go to my office."

Everybody agreed it was a good idea.

When we got home, I saw the cat had indeed gone. "Persnickle will be happy that Lucifer isn't in the house anymore," I said. "He sure was scared of that cat."

"Weren't we all!" Oleander said. "He seems to have taken a strange liking to Max, though."

I was only half listening, because I was busying myself making the coffee. "I'm dreading having dinner with Max's relatives again tonight," I admitted. "I'd be nervous enough just with his parents, but that Tabitha—she's something else."

"She might harbour resentment that Persnickle disrobed her and ate her clothes," Athanasius said.

"Undoubtedly." I handed him a cup of coffee. "I've been thinking about Walsh. If he's been in town for ages, he can't be a candidate to be a witch. We'll have to figure out how we can question him."

Oleander nodded. "I was thinking about that too. Goldie, you can go and visit him and say now that Sheila McFeeler has gone, you feel the anti-coffee law could be opposed successfully and chat to him on that basis. He might open up to you."

"But even if he does, he's not going to confess to her murder. What can I possibly find out from him?"

I handed Oleander her cup of coffee.

"Thanks," she said. "Look, Goldie, I have no idea what Walsh might tell you, but I'm sure he'll tell you something, and you won't know what he's going to tell you until you try. He won't think you suspect him. What's more, it's highly doubtful that he's a witch, so you won't be in danger from him at all. Especially when he thinks you're on his side over the coffee law."

"What if Max catches me talking to him?" I said.

"You do have a legitimate reason this time," Athanasius pointed out. "Max knows how much you like your coffee."

"That's true. I haven't been to Walsh's café yet, since it doesn't serve coffee. What's the point? I don't go to any East Bucklebury cafés, not unless I have to meet somebody. I did notice that it opened last week."

"Yes, well, when we get to the office, we'll mind it, and you can pop over and speak to him. At least, Max will be busy with his relatives."

"There is that," I said.

Persnickle was already asleep in his wombat bed, so three of us let ourselves out.

When I got to the office, I found a lot of junk mail strewn over my welcome mat. I picked one up and said a few rude words.

"What is it?" Oleander asked me.

"It's from a real estate agent from the Gold

Coast. Imagine leaving sales material on another agent's doorstep."

"They just pay people to do it," Athanasius said. "They wouldn't know."

"I know that, but it irritated me," I said, "and it's glary today."

Oleander chuckled. "It's always glary. It *is* Queensland, after all."

I pulled my sunglasses off my head and stuck them on my face, even though I was about to walk into my office. The landline was ringing, so I sprinted over to answer it. It was a conveyancer complaining that the bank refused to go to Tamborine Mountain to settle on the house I had just sold. The fee was going to be twenty-five dollars, and the sellers had refused to pay. I suggested to the conveyancer that the buyer pay. I don't know why they involved me.

"What was all that about?" Oleander said.

I relayed the gist of the conversation, and then added, "It's nothing to do with me. I'm just the selling agent. I think the person who called me is new at the lawyer's office and maybe doesn't know what they're doing. I hope my day improves," I said darkly.

I heard a crack of thunder in the distance.

"Calm down, Goldie," Oleander said. "You're brewing up a storm."

I nodded. "Maybe I should try to relax and watch a guided meditation on YouTube," I said. I pulled out my flask of coffee. "Maybe, I should sip coffee and do a guided meditation. That sounds relaxing."

Oleander and Athanasius exchanged glances.

CHAPTER 8

I had never been inside Walsh's café before. I had been inside the old one, which had been dark but at least had a pleasant atmosphere. Even from the outside, I could see Walsh had overturned the tranquil vibe. The front wall was painted orange, and a sign in garish fluorescent lime green announced the new name of the café, East Bucklebury Café. I considered it was a most unimaginative name. Still, it was on the main road through East Bucklebury so would get a lot of passing tourist traffic.

Sheila McFeeler's tearoom, as far as I could tell from looking through the windows, was indeed cozy and pretty with vintage décor, and vintage teapots and cups were dotted everywhere around.

I walked into the café and was dismayed to see that the interior was as unattractive as the exterior. Bright orange and metal seats surrounded the wooden tables I had remembered from the older café. I wondered if Walsh was colour-blind or whether he had just wanted to skimp on costs.

A smiling waitress looked up at me from behind the counter. "What can I get for you?"

"I'd like to speak to Walsh, if he's free."

"I'll just check." She disappeared from sight. I walked further into the café, noticing that the view here was indeed good, the sparkling sea through walls of glass. It was certainly a good position.

"Hello?" a deep voice said from behind me.

I spun around. Walsh looked like a semi-attractive Hollywood actor. He was tall, dark, and slim, with a dishevelled look that seemed deliberate. Musk, sandalwood, and vetiver notes of expensive men's cologne emanated from him in waves.

"Walsh? I've seen you around town. I'm Goldie Bloom." I would have said more, but he interrupted me.

"Yes, the real estate agent. You opened your office not far from here."

He reached out his hand, and I shook it. His grip was firm but not crushing.

He quirked one eyebrow. "What can I do for you?"

"I'm opposed to the anti-coffee law in town," I told him. "I'm sure it's affecting the price of houses in this town."

His face lit up. "Good. Come over here." He beckoned me to the back of the room and indicated I should sit at a small table right by the windows that afforded a wonderful view of the coastline. "Can I get you a cup of tea?"

"Ugh," I said. "Thanks, but no thanks."

He gave me a big wink. "How would you like your *tea*?"

I took his meaning at once. "Strong and black, please."

He disappeared and returned with a teacup in which was a deep black liquid. I could smell the delightful aroma of caffeine from across the room.

"Thank you," I said and immediately sipped it. "That's good, um, *tea*."

He laughed. "I mean, what a ridiculous bylaw! Nobody in their right mind would want those laws upheld."

"Except someone who was about to open a tearoom to trade off the law," I said.

He nodded grimly. "Sheila McFeeler. Of course, she was going to oppose us trying to overturn the law, because she was going to make a lot of money out of it."

"You mean by focusing her attention on selling tea rather than coffee?"

He nodded. "Yes, if coffee continued to be illegal in town, then she could market her tearoom as a successful alternative. East Bucklebury is somewhat of a quirky place, and people would no doubt flock to her tearoom. At least, that's what she thought. So, she had a great deal of self-interest involved in supporting the old bylaw."

"Just how difficult do you think it will be to get that bylaw overturned?" I asked him.

"I asked my lawyer, and he said he thought it wouldn't be able to be done. He thought it would require an Act of Parliament, and we would have to lobby the Federal government. Still, he admitted it was out of his depth. The Town Council didn't want to get legally involved, so a few of us are going to lobby as citizens. We're having a meeting of business people to form an action committee and to finalise the protest rally. Would you like to attend our meeting?"

"I'd love to," I said with enthusiasm.

Walsh looked pleased. However, my enthusiasm was at the thought of a whole lot of suspects being gathered into the one place. I wouldn't have to go looking for them. "So, have you actually formed a committee yet?" I asked him, confident he would think my interest was purely in overturning the antiquated anti-coffee bylaw.

"We're working towards that at the moment," he said. "Of course, it's going to be harder with the police sniffing around."

I feigned surprise. "The police?"

"Haven't you heard?" he said. "The police said Sheila McFeeler was murdered." He shot me a long hard look. "Aren't you friends with that detective?"

"I am," I admitted, "but he doesn't tell me anything police-related. He has a thing about it." I rolled my eyes. "Are you sure she was murdered? I thought her car hit a tree."

He looked around the room and spoke in a conspiratorial tone. "It's all over town—her brake lines were cut."

I gasped and did my best to look surprised. "You're kidding! Who do you think did it?"

He leant across the table. "No idea, but the police think it was one of us."

"Us?" I echoed.

"They seem to think it was another business in town, someone who opposed Sheila McFeeler over the coffee issue."

"But that's surely not a motive for murder. Was Sheila rich? Maybe her heirs murdered her."

He tapped his chin. "That's a point, but I don't think she was rich. Anyway, she was a very annoying woman, so she probably had made at least one bad enemy somewhere down the line."

"Hasn't she been in town for years?" I asked him.

He nodded. "Yes, although she left for a time before coming back. She sure annoyed a lot of people."

"And was she always in support of the anti-coffee law?"

He shook his head. "Well, if she was, she never said so before, not until recently when she was going to open her tearoom. The nerve of that woman!" He banged his fist on the table, startling me. Just then, his phone rang. He looked at me. "Sorry, I have to get this."

He looked out the window and spoke into the phone. "Hi, I'm just in a meeting right now. I'll call you later. Did you get home okay? How was the traffic on the M1?" He nodded and then hung up. "That was my girlfriend," he told me. "She lives in Brisbane. She was staying with me for a few days and went back this morning."

"That's nice," I said absently. "When is this meeting?"

"Tomorrow night at six, and it's in here," he said. "So, you can come for sure?"

I nodded. "Yes, I'm very keen to meet everyone." That, at least, was the truth. I took another gulp of coffee. "This is really good. Are you going to be able to make a living if the law isn't overturned?"

His face turned an ugly shade of red. "I don't see how. The lack of coffee in this town isn't a well-known fact. People come here and ask for coffee and then when we explain about the law, most of them get angry and they storm out, or they ask where the nearest town with coffee is. People take their coffee seriously, you understand."

"Believe me, I do understand."

"And as much as I disliked the woman, I have to admit that her idea of a tearoom was a clever idea, positioning her brand around the *lack* of coffee."

"Is anybody going to take over her business now she's gone?"

He looked surprised. "You know, I haven't thought of that."

"If you don't mind me asking, why did you buy this café if you knew you wouldn't be able to sell coffee?"

He leant across the table. "Because I thought the bylaw might possibly be overturned."

I raised my eyebrows. "Wasn't that a huge gamble? Especially after your lawyer told you it might require an Act of Parliament?"

"Nobody makes serious money without taking risks," he said smugly. "I got this café for a song. At the very least, it will pay its way, so I won't be going backwards with the finances, and I could make a lot of money. It's a good position here"— he gestured expansively and—"and we would serve good coffee. I thought it was a sensible business decision, certainly worth the risk."

"That's very clever of you," I said, thinking it wasn't clever at all. I'm sure if the anti-coffee bylaw could possibly be overturned, it would have been overturned by now, but I kept my opinions to myself. "Well, I certainly hope I'm not interviewed by the police over Sheila McFeeler's death," I added, in an attempt to bring the subject back to the murder victim.

He looked surprised. "Why would they question you?"

"Because I did tell her I didn't approve of her actions," I lied. "I mean, what is a town without coffee? I find the whole thing preposterous." He simply smiled and nodded. I pushed on. "I hope they catch the murderer soon, so they won't bother us."

"Still, the publicity will be good," Walsh said.

I raised one eyebrow. "How do you figure that?"

"Well, it was something my girlfriend said," he told me. "She works in business branding and marketing. She said that Sheila's death would attract a lot of publicity about the town and bring a lot of attention to the anti-coffee bylaw. She said it would rally public opinion against it, and it would also bring attention to the current cafés in town. I've already had a call from a Sydney paper wanting to interview me."

"That's fantastic," I said. "Do you think the publicity will continue after they catch the murderer?"

Once more, Walsh's face turned deep red. "Um, er, I don't know," he sputtered.

CHAPTER 9

I tried to talk myself into getting out of the bath, but the water was so deliciously warm. Besides, I was dreading meeting with Max's parents again. The four of them were going out to dinner with me—Max, Jack, Delilah, and Tabitha. I needed to make a good impression, especially after Persnickle had attacked Tabitha for wearing orange pyjamas. I didn't know how to make amends for that little incident, but I knew I had to give it my best shot.

Sighing, I stepped from the bath, wrapped a towel around myself, and tried to let out the bath water. Try as I might, I could not get the plug open. It was not a plug you plucked out of the bath, but the kind you pushed down a little so it would pop back up. I slammed the heel of my hand against my forehead. It was the seal! The old rubber seal had broken, and I had bought the wrong seal to replace it. Now I could not get the water to drain.

"Hello?" I hissed into the phone after it had chirped. It was Athanasius.

"You sound stressed," he said.

"I have this dinner thing with Max's parents tonight. Also, I need a seal urgently," I replied. I felt bad for hissing. It was just that I felt so embarrassed. What if Max's parents came home to my place after dinner and needed to use my bathroom and saw that the bath was full of water?

"You need a seal urgently?" He sounded puzzled.

"Yes! It's urgent!"

"How urgent?"

"Extremely urgent! Now would be great," I said more to myself than to Athanasius.

"I'm on it," he replied, and he hung up the phone.

I wondered where he would get a seal at this time of night. I hadn't even told him the size, and the hardware had a wide range of sizes. At any rate it was too late; the store would be closed. But

I didn't have time to think about this for long. The doorbell rang, and I scrambled to get ready.

"It's rude to leave one's guests waiting," Tabitha said as I brushed passed her. Jack and Delilah followed with sheepish smiles. For some reason, Max had decided that the five of us would go to the restaurant together in his car. I found myself wedged between Tabitha and Delilah in the back seat, praying I wouldn't get motion sickness and throw up on Tabitha's orange boots.

"Okay, folks," Max said as he pulled into the restaurant. I found myself gasping for breath as I crawled out of the car. Tabitha had doused herself in lavender perfume, and I suspected I was reacting to the chemicals.

"Wow, Goldie." Max grabbed my shoulders. "Maybe, you went a little overboard with the blush."

"I'm not wearing blush." It was true. I didn't have time to wear blush. I was too stressed about dinner and the seal.

"Maybe, we should go to the hospital," Max said gently. He pointed to the car window, and I looked at myself in the mirror.

I was bright red! In fact, I was bright red *and* bumpy. It had only taken five minutes of sitting next to Tabitha for my skin to erupt in hives. I went to scratch my face, but Max pinned my hands to my sides.

"No," he said. "You'll make things worse."

"I can't be seen looking like this," I cried softly.

"I see no difference in your appearance," Tabitha said. "And I'll not miss out on my dinner just because you are throwing another one of your tantrums."

I raised my eyebrows. "Another one of my…"

"That's enough, Tabitha," Max said.

Tabitha's mouth formed a perfect O. "How dare you," she sneered. "How dare…"

"Let's just get some dinner, shall we?" I said hurriedly. I yanked Max away from his wicked stepmother and dragged him into the restaurant. Soon, the five of us were sitting at a table in the centre of the room as I tried to ignore the stares.

It was probably the stress. The stress and the perfume. That's why I had broken out in hives. Now, if I could just get through tonight's dinner, then I would be okay. That's all I needed to do. Get through tonight's dinner without another hiccup.

I looked up to see Oleander and Athanasius pressing their faces against the window. They looked like children being very naughty. My eyebrows went so high they nearly touched my hairline, which would perhaps soon be receding from stress. What on earth were they doing? At least Max, Jack, Tabitha, and Delilah all had their backs to the window and could not see them.

"I'll just be a moment," I said, and I placed my napkin on the table.

Max looked concerned. "Are you all right?"

"Would you order for me?"

"Sure."

I thanked him. I pretended I was heading for the bathroom, but at the last moment I turned right and ran outside. "What on earth are you both doing?" I asked them.

"We got you a seal," Athanasius said proudly. He was positively beaming.

"Thank you," I said. "But couldn't this wait?"

"You said you needed a seal urgently."

"Not this urgently. When did you even get a seal at this time? All the stores are closed."

"From the local seal rescue," Oleander said, like this was obvious.

"What? The local seal rescue?" I repeated. "What, no. I need a seal for the bath!"

"Most people just get rubber ducks," Oleander said.

I frowned. "You stole a seal from the seal rescue?" I couldn't believe what I was hearing. "Where is the seal now?"

"At Walsh's house," Athanasius replied. "Oleander took the Retirement Home bus. We broke in and left the seal in his living room. Don't worry. We turned the television on for the little guy. He's watching *The Bachelor*."

"This cannot be happening," I muttered more to myself than to Oleander and Athanasius. "Why on earth is the seal at Walsh's?"

"Because we couldn't get into your house, so we figured if we just left the seal at Walsh's while he was out for the evening, then we could grab the seal when we went over there to investigate, which we should do right now," Oleander said.

"We are not breaking into Walsh's house to investigate him."

"But he's a suspect."

"And I'm having dinner with Max's family!"

"Everything okay?" Max poked his head around the restaurant door. "Your food is getting cold, Goldie."

"Yes," I said hurriedly. "Thank you."

"Hi, Oleander. Hi, Athanasius," Max said, before going back inside.

"You don't need to wear so much blush to impress Max," Oleander said.

"This is not happening." I scratched my skin. "Fine. We'll go to Walsh's, investigate, and get the seal, which you will then return to the seal rescue. Got it?"

"But I volunteer at the seal rescue on Tuesdays," Oleander said, as if that somehow made things better.

"But what about your bath?" Athanasius said.

"I'll get that rubber duck."

It did not take long for us to reach Walsh's. His house was on the water, and the back door was already unlocked, thanks to Oleander and Athanasius breaking in earlier that night.

I grabbed Oleander's arm. "How do you know Walsh isn't home?"

"Oleander swung by his café and stole his planner this morning. He is out at a friend's house until late tonight," Athanasius said.

I made a mental note to keep my belongings away from any octogenarian pickpockets. "Let's just get the seal, have a quick look around, and then leave," I said.

Oleander showed me into the living room, where the seal was happily lying on the floor. He had big eyes and long whiskers, and it looked as though he was grinning. Oleander bent down and scratched his stomach.

"The poor little guy is probably frightened," I muttered.

"Hardly. He's loving the trip away from the seal rescue. Aren't you, buddy?" Oleander chuckled as the seal thumped his short tail. "I'll load him into the car."

"How on earth will you do that?"

"He likes treats." Oleander reached into her purse and pulled out a packet of salmon slices.

"I think he likes them," I said, as I left to find Athanasius.

Walsh's kitchen was done up like a diner from the fifties. The tiles on the floor were black and white, while the walls were painted baby pink. The chairs at the dining table were turquoise. I noticed that Walsh's girlfriend had left a lot of things lying around, from dresses to jewellery to books.

"Athanasius?" I called out as I carefully trod up the stairs. "Please tell me there are no other animals here."

"Just the lion."

"What?"

"Kidding." Athanasius said as he emerged from a room. "I don't think Walsh is a witch. I don't see an altar. There is nothing witchy here at all."

"Good," I replied. "Then I can get back to that dinner."

"Don't you need to go to the hospital?"

"No, I've just had a bad reaction to Tabitha's perfume."

"Are you sure you haven't just had a bad reaction to Tabitha?" Athanasius asked.

"Well, that too."

Athanasius and I found Oleander in the car with the seal, whose name, she told me, was Clyde. Clyde was in the back seat with me, and he kept trying to shove past me to stick his head out the window, which was closed.

"Can you drop me off at the restaurant?" I asked.

"You don't want to take Clyde home?"

I felt my stomach knot. "No, I need to get back to Max."

Thankfully, neither Oleander nor Athanasius argued. After saying goodbye to them—and Clyde—I jumped from the car and burst into the restaurant. I threw myself into my seat, panting, and shook my head discreetly at Max. He could ask questions later. Just not in front of his family.

"I have digestion issues too," Delilah said kindly, and she grasped my hand.

"Oh, no. I wasn't in the bathroom."

"Then where, pray tell, were you?" Tabitha scoffed.

"Returning a seal that was taken from the seal rescue," I said.

Jack and Delilah laughed, but Max and Tabitha looked at me with intention. Tabitha, because she did not like me, and Max, because he knew me well enough to know I was up to no good.

"Can we have a word?" Max asked.

"Now you'll disappear for half an hour, too," Tabitha said. "Just what kind of family have I married into here?"

"The kind that minds their own business," Max said, as he dragged me over to a huge potted palm. "You better not have been investigating."

"Why would I have been investigating Walsh?"

"I didn't say Walsh."

"Excuse me?" I said faintly.

Max folded his arms. "I didn't say anything

about Walsh. I hope you haven't been harassing him."

"I didn't go near the man," I said, which was true.

"I'm a detective, I..."

"A very dashing detective," I corrected him.

"I can't have my girlfriend doing anything illegal." He was frustrated.

"Like, breaking and entering?"

"Exactly."

"Good to know," I said. "I am glad we've cleared that up, Detective Grayson."

"I don't want to arrest you, but I will do my duty if I am forced."

"Meaning?"

"I *will* arrest you."

"Can I put the lights on in your police car? And the siren?"

"Obviously."

"You would never arrest me," I said then.

Max grinned. "I know."

I checked to make sure Tabitha was not staring at us, and I reached out to squeeze his hand. "I will tell you everything in good time. For now, can you please help me impress your parents?"

"I've been trying to impress them for years."

"Then you've had a lot of practice."

"And very little success."

"Shall we make it a team effort then?"

Max offered me his arm. "I think we shall."

The two of us returned to the table, grinning from ear to ear.

CHAPTER 10

*O*leander knocked on my door. "Max is here."

I was getting ready to go to the meeting at Walsh's café. I hurried into the living room, tying my bathrobe tightly around me. Thank goodness the bath now had a seal, a rubber one at that.

"Are you going out?" Max asked me.

"Yes, to the meeting in Walsh's café," I said. "He's having a meeting for people who will oppose the anti-coffee law."

Max looked decidedly put out. "I didn't know you opposed the law."

I gestured to my kitchen. "Are you kidding? You know I have an illegal coffee machine in there. Of course, I'm opposed to the anti-coffee law."

Max narrowed his eyes. "Obviously, you want coffee to be legal in this town, Goldie, but you haven't actually been an activist before."

"Yes, but thinking what happened to Sheila McFeeler made me consider the matter," I said. "Maybe, real estate prices in this town will go up if coffee is legal, and besides, Walsh invited me to the meeting."

Max put his hands on his hips. "Did he now?"

"How are things with your parents and your stepmother going, Max?" Oleander asked him.

I shot her a grateful look for changing the subject.

"As well as can be expected," Max said. He sounded wary.

"Is Tabitha giving you a hard time?" I asked him.

"Tabitha gives everyone a hard time, even my father," Max said. "I really don't know what he sees in that woman. I have no idea how she got him under her spell."

"It wasn't her personality," Athanasius muttered, followed by, "Sorry."

"Have you made any headway into the murder investigation yet?" I asked him.

Max sighed. "No, and if I did, I wouldn't tell you."

I pouted.

"Now, Goldie, don't look at me like that. Put the murder out of your mind."

"But how can she?" Oleander said. "Athanasius and I are staying here until the murderer is found. Safety in numbers, and all that."

"But surely you're safe at the retirement home," Max said, "unless you're afraid a senior citizen is the murderer."

Oleander frowned. "Now, there's no need to be ageist, Max. What if the murderer strikes again? We are staying here to keep Goldie safe. If you catch the murderer, please let us know and then we can go back to the retirement home."

"I certainly will tell you when we catch the murderer," Max said.

"Sheila said her son inherits everything," I told him.

Max looked shocked, and I realised my mistake. "I thought you didn't know her?"

"I didn't know her, but I have spoken to her," I said.

Max shot me a suspicious look.

"Are you having dinner with your parents again tonight?" Oleander asked Max.

"Yes. Well, I had better leave. They're coming over to my house tonight and I'm making dinner for them. Are you sure you can't come, Goldie? Oh, and Oleander and Athanasius, you're most welcome too."

"I do have to go to the meeting," I said. I looked at Oleander.

"Athanasius and I need to mind Persnickle. How is Lucifer doing?"

Max ran a hand over his forehead. "How did you know the cat's name?"

Oleander smiled. "I remembered I'd heard Sheila mention it once."

Max seemed to swallow her story. "I think he dislikes Tabitha as much as Persnickle does. That sure is one feisty cat."

"He seems to like you," I pointed out.

Max nodded. "That's the main thing. He did take an instant liking to me. Maybe, he'll grow to like others in time."

Oleander and I exchanged glances. "Well, sorry to rush off, but I'll be late for the meeting if I don't throw on some clothes," I said.

"Don't throw on any clothes on my account," Max said with a big wink.

"You're forgetting you have an audience in the room," Oleander said in a lecturing tone.

I reached up and gave Max a light kiss before running back into my room. I finished applying my make-up and then put on my clothes. I was fairly certain the murderer would be at the meeting tonight—that was, of course, unless the murderer was a witch.

When I came out, Oleander caught my arm. "Before you rush off Goldie, there's something I've been meaning to ask you, and it can't wait."

"You can eat all the rum balls in the fridge," I said.

She shook her head. "Too late. Athanasius already ate them. No, it's not that. If there was another witch around, would you feel it?"

I was puzzled and I said so. "What do you mean?"

"Would you sense it on some type of psychic or intuitive level? If a witch was in town to murder you, would you feel something was amiss?"

I thought about it. "I have felt uneasy for the last few days, but I thought it was simply because I was nervous about meeting Max's family."

"Then think about it now," Athanasius said. "Do you think it could be something else?"

I shut my eyes and considered the matter. After a few moments, I opened them. "Yes, you know, you could be right. I *do* feel under some kind of threat. It's hard to explain, but I kind of feel like I'm holding myself tightly. I can't explain it, because it's a spiritual feeling."

Oleander tut-tutted. "So, you do think there could be a witch in town who means you harm?"

I nodded slowly. "Quite possibly, but on the other hand, it could just be that I'm nervous about Max's parents, and it hasn't gone well right from the time I met them. It's that dreadful woman with her orange hair."

"Tomorrow, why don't we take Persnickle and you can speak with Sheila's ghost again," Oleander said. "Ask her if she had the feeling too."

I grabbed my car keys. "But wouldn't she have told us if she did?"

Oleander shook her head. "No, because you weren't aware of it until we asked you. Maybe, it just hadn't occurred to her, and she needs to think about it first."

"That's true. Well, I had better get to the

meeting because if it was a mundane reason for murder, then people there would have had a motive." I hurried out the door with a wave over my shoulder.

"Test your brakes as soon as you leave," Athanasius called after me.

I drove down the road a short way and tested my brakes. They worked fine. I drove a little further and tested them again. So far, so good. Since Sheila McFeeler's death, I had been keeping my car in my lock-up garage instead of in the carport outside it, but I was certain that a determined murderer could find their way into the garage.

I had no idea what I was looking for at the meeting tonight. I tested my brakes again and thought about it some more. Motives. Yes, that's what I was looking for, motives.

I still hadn't had a chance to check to see whether Sheila's son was, in fact, a rich businessman living in Dubai. He stood to inherit everything.

I thought about her house. It wasn't on the water, and without any research, I guessed that would be worth around six hundred thousand dollars. I had no idea how much money she had in the bank, and I had no idea how big her mortgage was or even whether she had one. She had lived in East Bucklebury for some time, so maybe if she did have a mortgage, it was a tiny one. Twenty years ago, East Bucklebury didn't even have sewerage and the houses were very cheap indeed. It was a backwater and not a tourist destination until a big company had come to town and turned the swampland on the ocean to luxury homes, charging well over one million dollars per home. They had seen to it that sewerage was introduced to town, but all the residents were still dependant on tank water.

When I got to Walsh's café, I had to park up the road because plenty of cars were parked outside already. It certainly looked as though the meeting was going to be a popular one. My stomach clenched as I thought that I would possibly meet the murderer tonight. I also told myself to keep my psychic feelers on full alert for any witchy vibes.

When I walked into the café, Walsh met me at the door. He handed me a brochure. "Good to see you, Goldie. I'm glad you could come," he said. "We're going to have a meeting, and then will have a cup of *tea* afterwards." When he said the word *tea*, he winked at me.

I sat at the back of the room and took out a pen and notepad, ostensibly to take notes about the meeting but in fact to take notes about the people present. I recognised the marina owners and several other storekeepers.

Soon, Walsh took the floor. He explained at length, repeating his lawyer's words about possibly needing an Act of Parliament to overturn the anti-coffee bylaw. He suggested he should take up a collection to pay for the services of a good Brisbane lawyer. Judging by the murmurs of agreement, it didn't seem as though his plan would attract any objections.

Walsh also suggested forming a committee and action group. Everyone put up their hands, while I looked down at my notepad and studiously avoided eye contact.

Despite the meeting being about coffee, one of my favourite subjects, it soon got boring. At first, Walsh mentioned some other interesting antiqued bylaws. He said it was illegal in Victoria to touch a high-voltage electric wire that caused instant death, as this would attract a two hundred dollar fine. It was also illegal to dress as Batman or Robin in that state. All Aussie bars are legally required to provide a stable, hay, and water for their customers' horses. However, I lost interest when Walsh droned on and on about the technicalities of Acts of Parliament.

I was glad when he brought the meeting to an end, but my relief was short lived because he said, "Are there any questions?"

I wanted to ask when the meeting would be over but fought the urge.

A woman from the front row waved her hand vigorously. "Do you think Sheila McFeeler's death will attract sympathy to her cause?"

"I'll let Madison answer that," Walsh said.

A slim, well-dressed woman walked over to stand next to Walsh. "It's possible, but I'm keeping a watch on the media. If that appears in any of the papers, I'll make sure I shut it down quickly. So far, the media seems firmly on our side in our coffee wars."

There were a few more questions, but I simply sat there, wondering who the woman was until it dawned on me. Madison must be Walsh's girlfriend, the one from Brisbane.

After Madison spoke for a full five minutes, there were no further questions. Walsh suggested he form a Facebook group and invite us all. We all joined the group on our phones then and there. "And now that the doors are locked and the curtains are drawn, we can all have coffee," Walsh said to the sound of cheers.

At that time of night, I would have preferred wine, but I wasn't one to refuse a cup of coffee.

A short lady walked over to me. "You're the new real estate agent in town, aren't you?" she asked.

I studied her. Her face was round and plump but covered with worry lines, and her eyes were sad. "Yes, but I've been in town for a while. Of course, I know I have to be third-generation in a country town for someone to think I'm a local," I said.

She laughed long and hard. When she finished laughing, she said, "I'm Dolly Florette, and that's my husband, Boris, over there talking to Madison."

"Is Madison Walsh's girlfriend?"

Dolly nodded.

"She's in marketing, I believe?"

"Yes, she is very smart."

"Weren't you the lady who owned the café before Walsh bought it? I'm sure I saw you in here when I met with clients on occasion."

Dolly nodded. "That's right. Boris and I owned it. We sold it to Walsh for a pittance. He certainly has changed the decor." Her nose wrinkled in disgust.

I lowered my voice and leant forward. "I much preferred your decor."

Dolly nodded. "Me too. Boris is quite angry about how it looks now, but he's not one to say anything. He just broods on things and gets very angry."

"He's angry about the decor?" I asked her.

She nodded and then shook her head. "Well sort of, but he's mainly angry that we sold the café for chickenfeed to Walsh. It's not Walsh's fault, mind you—we weren't able to sell it to anybody else. It was on the market for a long time. Who can sell a café in a town where coffee is illegal?"

I opened my mouth to say something, but she pushed on. "We tried to keep the place afloat you see, with sandwiches and stuff like that and cold drinks, but when that, that…"—she hesitated—"dreadful woman came out so strongly in support of the anti-coffee law, we knew it was the end for us. Boris was very upset."

"Boris was very upset with Sheila McFeeler?"

"Yes. I mean, it was clever on her part to plan a tearoom in a town where coffee was illegal. All the tourists would flock there."

"But wouldn't they be angry that they couldn't get coffee? Sure, I realise she was going to open a tearoom, but I've been in tearooms in England and they still sell coffee."

Dolly shook her head. "No, no, no. She was going to market herself in a big way and say she only had tea. It was all part of her marketing plan. Madison told me."

"Did Madison know Sheila?" I thought it was rather strange if she had.

Dolly looked puzzled. "I don't think so, but Madison is in marketing, and it got back to her that Sheila had hired a marketing company to brand her business. Sheila thought she was going to make a lot of money out of it. She didn't care who she stomped on, people like me and people like Boris."

"Oh yes, it must have been awful for you."

"I hope her son doesn't want to carry on the business," Dolly said, rubbing her forehead hard.

"Her son? I heard he was a rich businessman in Dubai."

Dolly drained her coffee and then stuffed a

strawberry iced doughnut in her mouth. She took some time to eat it, and I was consumed with curiosity. I tapped my foot impatiently. Finally, she spoke. "No, no, no. He *was* a rich businessman, but he has a gambling problem. He went broke. He isn't in Dubai, either—he's living at the Gold Coast. I saw him at Pacific Fair only the other week. He asked me not to tell his mother he was in town."

"And did you tell her?"

Dolly's fists clenched and unclenched. "No way! I wasn't going to tell that, that... woman anything! If her son wanted his privacy, then he was entitled to have it."

I remembered his name was Tristan Smith. "Is Smith his father's surname?" I asked her.

Dorothy's features relaxed and she gave a little chuckle. "Sheila's family was obviously bad with names. I mean, Sheila McFeeler! Wouldn't you change your name if your name was Sheila McFeeler?" Before I could respond, she continued. "And she called her cat Lucifer! Who calls a cat Lucifer? No, Tristan legally changed his name to Tristan Smith."

"Was he born Tristan?" I asked her.

She nodded. "Yes, he was born Tristan

McFeeler, and he changed it to Tristan Smith years ago. Oh look, here's Boris now."

Boris wasn't much taller than Dolly. He had an affable smile, and I couldn't imagine him having a temper.

"Dolly was just explaining to me that the two of you owned this café and sold it to Walsh," I said.

Any doubts I had about him not having a temper soon fled. His face turned as red as an angry ripe tomato. I am sure ripe tomatoes couldn't be angry, but if they could, then they would have looked exactly like Boris at that moment. "That blasted woman," he said through clenched teeth. "I'd tell you what I thought of her, but I can't because you're a lady and my wife is present too, so I will just have to keep my opinions to myself."

"I'm terribly sorry about what she did to you," I said lamely. I was at a loss as to what to say.

"Karma!" Boris suddenly exclaimed, causing me to jump.

"Excuse me?"

"Karma! Do you believe in karma?"

"Um, er," I sputtered, but he pushed on.

"Karma got that woman. Not that I would

wish anyone dead," he added as an afterthought, although he was clearly lying. It was clear to me that Boris very much wanted Sheila McFeeler dead, and I imagined so did his wife, although she was less forthcoming about it.

CHAPTER 11

The following morning, I got up early and staggered into the kitchen like a zombie, my hands extended in front of me, searching for the coffee pot. I got the coffee ready and then heard a grunt behind me.

I swung around to see Oleander.

"You look like a zombie," she said.

I grunted. "Have you looked in the mirror? And is Athanasius awake yet?"

"After I have some coffee, I'll knock on his door."

"Did somebody mention my name?" said a male voice from the doorway. Athanasius tottered into the kitchen.

"You know, I wonder how all those law-abiding, non-coffee drinking citizens manage in the mornings," I said. "I can't imagine how anyone could live without a drop of caffeine in their bloodstreams."

Oleander, Athanasius, and even Persnickle all grunted in response.

Persnickle looked bleary-eyed. "You can have an early breakfast for once," I told him, "but don't get into the habit of demanding it at six in the morning."

Persnickle ate his breakfast before waddling out of the room. I stuck my head around the kitchen door to see he had headed straight back to his wombat bed and had probably fallen asleep. I hoped I wasn't going to have any trouble getting him in the car at this early hour.

"Are you sure Max won't catch us if we go this early?" Oleander asked me.

"I don't think he's following me, and he has his hands full with his relatives. He won't suspect we're going back to the crash scene today. He has no idea I'm a sea witch and I can speak to ghosts with the help of Persnickle."

Athanasius chuckled, but Oleander said, "When are you going to tell him?"

I clutched my stomach. "When the relationship is a little more advanced. It's not something I can bring up easily."

Athanasius and Oleander nodded solemnly. After we each had three cups of coffee, we all felt sufficiently caffeinated to leave the house. I clicked Persnickle's leash on him and said, "Ride in the car."

Persnickle did a happy dance.

At this hour, the traffic on the road to Brisbane was light. I was able to do a U-turn and pull off the road at the site of Sheila McFeeler's fatal car crash. Persnickle hopped out of the car nimbly. Oleander and Athanasius followed more slowly.

I walked over to the tree. "Sheila! Sheila McFeeler!" I called out. I looked around me. Nothing. "I don't think she's here," I told them.

"Maybe she has crossed over or gone towards the light or whatever ghosts do," Athanasius said.

Oleander shot him a glare. "That's not very helpful."

"It might not be helpful, but it might be a fact."

"She's possibly hanging around her house," I said. "I'll try here a bit longer, and then we will go to the house."

We stayed there another five minutes, which

was longer than I wanted to stay, but I wanted to be certain that the ghost wasn't going to appear before I left for her house. All the while, I was watching the road, hoping Max wouldn't catch me. Explaining why Persnickle had to have two bathroom breaks in exactly the same spot on different days with two barely explained trips to Brisbane would be way too much for Max to swallow.

"Okay, I give up. Let's head back to the car and go to her house," I said.

"What if she's in her tearoom?" Oleander asked me.

"It's going to be awfully difficult to take Persnickle there," I said. "I suppose I could walk him along the street past it and stop outside hoping she'll turn up, but I think the best bet is the house."

We drove to Sheila's house the back way. I was hoping I wouldn't run into any police, especially Max. Once more, we parked down the road amongst the mangroves and walked to the back door. I knocked loudly on the back door.

"Why did you knock?" Athanasius asked me. "Ghosts don't answer doors."

"Nope, but maybe her son or someone else

could be inside, and I can't call out for her ghost if somebody is there."

Athanasius nodded and opened his mouth to speak, but Sheila's ghost suddenly appeared. "What are you doing here?" she asked.

"She's here," I said to Oleander and Athanasius. To Sheila's ghost, I said, "I've come to speak to you, of course."

She nodded. "Do they know who murdered me yet?"

I shook my head. "But I wanted to discuss that with you. As you know, it was either a mundane murder or it was a witch who murdered you to get your powers. Did you feel anything magical or witchy around you, say the week or so leading up to your death?"

The ghost faded a little and then solidified. "What do you mean?"

"Well, did you get any psychic impressions that maybe somebody was against you? Did you feel under any threat? And if so, did it feel a magical threat or a mundane threat?"

She faded again. I thought she had gone, when she suddenly materialised, giving me a fright. "I did feel uneasy, but I thought it was just because of the trouble I was having with the people opposed to the anti-coffee law."

"If you look back, can you see if there was any magical attention on you, if you know what I mean?"

"I know what you mean." She shut her eyes tightly, and this time stayed materialised. "You know, I think you're right. I did feel as though there was another witch around, but only the day before I died. It was the same feeling I'd felt on previous occasions, but only for a few days at a time."

"Can you get a handle on the type of feeling?" I pressed her.

Once more, she shut her eyes tightly. "It was as though there was another witch around, but like I said, the feeling didn't stay." She tapped her chin. I wondered why her finger didn't pass through her, given that she was a ghost. "The feeling was there again the day before the accident, but I suppose I didn't think anything of it since I'd felt it once or twice over the past year or so."

"Maybe, it was someone who comes to town on occasion," I said.

"Yes, it definitely wasn't a permanent resident, because there were times I didn't feel it at all, and

I didn't feel it on a very regular basis, just now and then."

"And when did this start?" I asked her.

"I'm not sure. Maybe a year ago? It might have been a bit longer. Anyway, I'm sure it wasn't as long as two years."

"Okay then, so we have someone who comes to town on occasion, that is, if it was a witch who killed you," I said. "And as for mundane suspects, did you have a particular run-in with Dolly and Boris Barrette?"

The ghost scowled. "Oh, yes. Walsh bought their café. Nasty people." Her face wrinkled with disgust.

"I thought Dolly seemed nice," I said.

The ghost grunted. "She *seems* nice all right, but she makes the bullets, and Boris fires them. She gets him all worked up about stuff, and he does her dirty work."

"Does Boris have a temper?"

She nodded. "Yes, he sure does."

Oleander interjected. "Boris does have a temper, Goldie. He and Dolly have been in town for years. He has a terrible temper."

To Oleander, I said, "Sheila agrees with you."

To Sheila, I said, "Then do you think Boris would have it in him to murder you?"

Athanasius stepped forward. "He used to be a mechanic, so he know how to cut brake lines."

"I'm not a mechanic, but I could probably find out how to cut brake lines," I said. "I could find something easily enough on YouTube. What sort of car did you have, Sheila?"

"A Toyota."

I turned to the others. "Sheila said she had a Toyota. It would be easy to know where the brake lines were in a Toyota. It's not as if it was some sort of exotic European car."

Oleander and Athanasius both nodded. "So, have you been thinking any more about it?" I asked the ghost. "Have you come up with any suspects?"

"I have been thinking about it, and nobody has been snooping around my house. I somehow ended up at my house and I've been here ever since. The police have been here once, but they didn't take long and that was all."

"If a witch murdered you, I wonder if they would want to take any of your stuff from the house?" I asked her.

The ghost shrugged. "I imagine stealing my powers was enough."

"Your powers!" I exclaimed.

"What did she say?" Oleander asked me

I shook my head. "It's not what she said—something just occurred to me. If a witch has taken Sheila's powers, we should keep our eye out for storms and suchlike. If something upsets a sea witch, then there will be a sudden thunderstorm or a hailstorm or something like that."

"But if the murderer thought there was another sea witch in town, they would be very careful to control their emotions, because they wouldn't want to give themselves away," Oleander pointed out.

"This is all making my head spin," I said. "It's too early in the morning to think."

"My son!" the ghost exclaimed. "What's he doing here?" With that, she vanished.

I turned around and saw a man walking around the corner towards us. He looked pleasant enough. He was about my height with sandy hair, and his complexion was pale. Judging by the scent of sandalwood, musk, and vetiver, he was wearing the same cologne as Walsh. "Hello?" he said. "What are you doing here?"

"Who are you?" Athanasius countered.

"I'm Tristan Smith." He strode over to us.

"Sheila's son," I said. He nodded. " I was a friend of your mother's," I said. "I'm Goldie Bloom, the local real estate agent, and these are my assistants, Oleander and Athanasius. We were coming to leave a note here. The local detective, Max Grayson, has your mother's cat at his place. We came to leave a note in case whoever came to look after mother's property was worried about the cat."

Tristan looked puzzled. "The cat?"

"Yes, Lucifer. You knew your mother had a cat?"

"Lucifer!" he spat. "What a ridiculous name for a cat. The whole family had ridiculous names."

"Then you don't want to keep the cat?"

"Of course not."

"The detective will be pleased to hear that. He's grown quite accustomed to that cat."

Tristan quirked an eyebrow. "The cat hasn't scratched him?"

"No, but he attacked everybody else," Oleander said, pointing to the Band-Aid that was still plastered across her forehead.

"Well, I'd ask you inside, but I just want to get

my mother's property wrapped up and sold," he said.

That was obviously a dismissal. "Max will be happy about the cat. Goodbye," I said.

The three of us were at the side of the building when he called after me. "Wait! Did you say you're a real estate agent?"

I stopped and turned around. "Yes."

"Can you put your number in my phone?" He handed me his phone, and I tapped my number into his contacts.

"I'm looking to get this house sold as soon as I can. I have to find out about probate and everything else."

"Are you the sole executor?"

He nodded.

"You might not need probate. Unless you need probate for some other reason, then you won't need it for the house, not in Queensland at any rate. You just have to get a Section 5a form and file it with the Registry office in Brisbane, and then you will become a representative of your mother's estate. Once that happens, it's just the same as selling any house."

His face lit up. "So, I don't need to wait months for probate?"

I shook my head. "No, not at all. That is, unless there is probate needed for some other legal reason, such as a certain amount in your mother's bank account and stuff like that. If your mother's bank account is over a certain monetary limit, you will need probate, but if it isn't, and you don't need probate otherwise, then you don't need it for the house. A lawyer can easily do it for you, or you can just fill out the Section 5a form and post it to the Department of Natural Resources, Mines, and Energy in Brisbane."

"If I give you the listing, would you explain it all to me later? I don't think I have enough money for a lawyer."

"Sure," I said. "I can explain it to you if you sign an exclusive listing with me."

He smiled broadly. "I'm glad we met." With that, he turned his back and busied himself unlocking the back door.

This time, we walked around to the front of the house and down the garden path, as it would have looked strange if we had walked out the back and headed into the mangrove swamp.

Persnickle busied himself eating all the plants flanking the footpath. I did my best to stop him, but I only saved a couple of orange clivia flowers.

When we were back in my car, both Athanasius and Oleander spoke excitedly. "Did you hear that?" Athanasius said. "He said he couldn't afford a lawyer! He must be completely broke. We have to look into this some more."

"Yes, money could well have been a motive for murder in his case," I said. "I wish we knew whether it was a mundane murder or a magical murder."

Just then, there was a crack of thunder, and the sky turned black. "It's a sea witch!" Oleander said. "Who else could do that? You're not upset, Goldie, so there *is* another sea witch in town. Something must have just happened to upset them. And they might be coming for you!"

CHAPTER 12

Persnickle and I were inside Oleander's apartment at the East Bucklebury Retirement Home. Actually, I was inside the apartment, while Persnickle was in the courtyard at the back, eating weeds and probably anything else he could get his teeth on.

Oleander was certain that some of the residents would be able to provide more information on the suspects. We were sitting in her small living room, all of us with pens hovering over our notepads.

Athanasius stood up abruptly. A lemon tart fell from his pocket. He bent down, picked it up, and placed it on the coffee table in front of him. "And now let's look at the suspects," he said. "Who do we have?"

"The victim's son, Tristan Smith," I said. "We need to look into him a lot more, given that he seems to be broke. I don't know how much money Sheila had in her bank account or whether or not she had a mortgage, but her house would be worth around six hundred thousand dollars. Plus, it doesn't have to be split with other siblings or heirs —Tristan is the sole beneficiary."

I stopped talking and wrote Tristan's name on my notepad.

"And there's Walsh, of course," Oleander said. "He bought that place for a song from Dolly and Boris Florette."

Athanasius shook his finger at her and then sat down. "And indeed, Dolly and Boris are prime suspects. They wouldn't have gone broke if it wasn't for the anti-coffee law."

I held up one finger in a gesture of objection. "But the anti-coffee law was here before they were born. Plus, I'm sure they would have been able to sell that café before Sheila moved back to town."

Oleander agreed with Athanasius. "Nevertheless, they are strong suspects. Who else do we have?"

"Madison, Walsh's girlfriend," I said.

Athanasius looked surprised. "Why her? Doesn't she live in Brisbane?"

I nodded. "I have her as a suspect for two reasons. Firstly, because she is Walsh's girlfriend, so any motives of his could also be hers, and also because she is possibly a witch. Remember that Sheila's ghost told me she felt a witchy presence on occasion in town, but she said it wasn't here all the time. That means the witch isn't a local."

"We didn't actually hear her, but you relayed what she said," Athanasius said.

Oleander rolled her eyes. "That's what Goldie meant."

Athanasius pouted. "Then why didn't she say so?"

I ignored him and asked, "Do we have any other suspects?"

They looked blank, so I added, "Let's write 'unknown witch' and add that to the suspects. I mean, if it was a witch who murdered Sheila, then we don't know the identity of that witch."

Oleander nodded slowly. "That's a good idea."

"And another idea occurred to me in the night," Athanasius said. "Whoever cut Sheila

McFeeler's brake lines must have known she was specifically driving to Brisbane on that road."

I didn't catch his meaning at first. "Why do you say that?"

"Because all the roads around here are flat. It's not as if she could have driven down a steep hill anywhere. The only possible way anybody who lived in these parts could be killed by brakes failing would be if they were out on that road. Otherwise, they would have had plenty of chances to test their brakes and find they weren't working. Sheila only had to drive straight down her road as it turned gently into the main road, no brakes required. That sharp bend where she did, in fact, die was on that main road."

"Of course!" I exclaimed. I dropped my pen in excitement and then bent down to pick it up. I saw a big dust bunny under the sofa and wondered if I should tell Oleander but then figured she would be embarrassed. I mean, who doesn't have dust bunnies under their sofas? I straightened up and said, "That's right! That must narrow it down. It was somebody who knew she was driving to Brisbane that day. As you said, Athanasius, cutting brake lines wouldn't have been fatal for anyone just driving around town, because everything here is so flat, and the speed limit is so low."

It was Oleander's turn to stand up. "Then who knew she was driving to Brisbane that day? And why was she driving to Brisbane?" She looked at me, and I shrugged.

"No idea," said Athanasius, "but that's something we need to find out."

"She might have been going to see a lawyer." I ran my hand over my forehead. "Well, there's no point indulging in idle speculation. We'll ask around."

"And there's something else that occurred to me, but you won't like it, Goldie." Athanasius's normally pale face grew even whiter.

I was alarmed. "What is it?"

"Max is a good detective, is he not?" I nodded. He pushed on. "Max hasn't solved the case yet or at least found any strong suspects."

"I don't know where you're going with this Athanasius, but Max wouldn't tell us if he had any suspects," Oleander pointed out.

Athanasius disagreed. "He is very protective of Goldie. So, if he did have a suspect, then he would tell her to stay away from whoever it was. No, I don't think he has a clue. And that leads me to believe that a witch is probably the perpetrator."

I gripped the edge of the sofa with both hands. "So, you really think it was a witch?" I squeaked.

"I'm afraid I do," Athanasius said, "and don't forget that storm suddenly came up last night. It does look as though there is another sea witch in town."

Oleander corrected him. "Not necessarily a sea witch, but a witch who has taken Sheila McFeeler's sea witch powers."

"If she has sea witch's powers, then she is now a sea witch."

I thought they might get into an argument about what a sea witch especially was or wasn't, so I hastened to add, "Well then, if it is a witch, we know it isn't Walsh, and it can't be Dolly or Boris either because they've been here for a long time too. Madison lives in Brisbane and Tristan Smith hasn't been living in East Bucklebury either. Both of them do come to town on occasion."

"So we have three witch suspects," Oleander said. "Tristan Smith, Madison, and 'unknown witch.' Of course, we don't know if Madison or Tristan are witches, but we need to put them on our witch suspect list. As for mundane suspects, we have Dolly and Boris, either working individually or together, and Walsh. We need to put Tristan Smith and Madison on the mundane suspect list as well. So, we have Walsh and Madison, either working individually or together."

I sighed long and hard. "This is mentally exhausting. We have too many suspects, and we haven't made any headway at all into the investigation. Like you said, Athanasius, the fact that Max apparently hasn't either makes me think a witch *is* involved. I'm going to have to increase magical protection around my house."

"I thought you would have done that already!" Oleander said, her hands flying to her cheeks.

"Yes I did, but I mean even more," I said. "I'm quite concerned about all this."

"Then we had better get moving on our investigation. Let's go and speak to the residents."

I walked outside to find Persnickle asleep in the sun. "Sorry to wake you, Persnickle," I said, reaching for him with the harness.

He became excited. "We're going to see the residents," I told him, hoping he wasn't disappointed not go for a ride in a car quite yet. I put on his therapy wombat blanket. Persnickle did a little wombat dance, as he knew that meant

Athanasius would give him a lemon tart. In fact, Athanasius paused halfway from Oleander's apartment to the main complex of the retirement home to do just that. Persnickle gobbled it up as we walked along.

We caught sight of some of the residents sitting under brightly coloured umbrellas in the courtyard, in which were beautiful tropical plants, gorgeous red and green cordylines, non-invasive bamboos, and brightly coloured begonias.

I sat down next to a large red and green neoregelia bromeliad plant and inhaled the heady scent of the jasmine bushes nearby. As soon as I looked up, I was dismayed to see Harriet Hemsworth. Worse still, she made a beeline for me, and she was clutching her dreadful book.

Harriet placed the heavy book on the table in front of us. It landed with a thud. "I have some wonderful photos of new diseased skin and ailments to show you," she said in a high-pitched voice. "I have a wonderful photo of a very diseased, dissected spleen."

I clutched my stomach and fought the wave of nausea that flooded over me. "Maybe later," I said. "I'm feeling a little sick in my stomach." That, at least, was the truth.

"Oh, then these photos will cheer you up," she said brightly.

Oleander came to my rescue. She leant across the table and said in a conspiratorial tone, "We are secretly investigating the murder of Sheila McFeeler."

Harriet looked even more pleased. "That's wonderful!" she exclaimed. "How can I help? Who do you suspect?"

"Can you think of anyone who would have wanted to kill her?" Oleander countered.

Harriet looked around the table. "Well, Boris Florette hated her, and he used to be a mechanic. He could have easily cut her brake lines."

"But I could probably cut someone's brake lines if I googled how to do it first," I said.

Harriet looked crestfallen. "But Boris does have rather serious anger management problems. He was a client of mine when I first came to town. Don't tell anyone, will you? I'm not supposed to do it anymore."

"He was?" I looked at her intently. Harriet had been a naturopath years ago, although she had been struck off. "Did he come to you for anger management problems?"

Harriet bit her lip and frowned hard. She didn't

speak for a few moments. Finally, she said, "Yes, he was a client of mine, but it would be breaching client confidence to tell you why I was treating him. Still, I can show you a photograph of his boil."

I covered my eyes with both hands. "Please don't!" I said weakly.

There was silence, so I opened my eyes. It was most unfortunate that I did so, because I looked straight at a photo of a dreadful boil. In fact, I even couldn't begin to describe what I saw. I shut my eyes tightly. "I can't look at that. I'm not feeling well," I said truthfully. "Oleander, tell me when she puts it away."

"I'm not looking either," she said.

"Athanasius?" I said hopefully.

"It's safe to look now," he said after an interval.

I carefully opened one eye and then the other one, and to my relief, the book was indeed shut. Harriet looked quite put out. "Why aren't you all excited to see my wonderful pictures?" she demanded. "They're very medically interesting and in colour! All the residents love seeing them. Why, I showed Enid Butler some of the new photos this morning, just before she fainted."

"Um, it's just that we need to focus on your sleuthing skills," I lied. "If Boris killed her, then what was his motive?"

Harriet leant across the table once more. "Dolly and Boris were going to sell their café last year." She hesitated and looked up to the sky before adding, "Or maybe it was the year before. Time flies, you know? I haven't been in town that long myself. Anyway, they were going to sell it to someone from the south Gold Coast for a good sum. They planned to retire on the proceeds, but there was all the buzz around town about the possibility of overturning the old coffee bylaw, so they hung onto the café. They thought they were going to make a go of it. But then, Sheila McFeeler came back to town with all her nonsense supporting the anti coffee bylaw. She sent them broke."

I interrupted her. "So, they would have made good money if they'd sold the café a year or two ago, but they hung on to it thinking the anti-coffee law would be overturned and ended up selling it to Walsh for a pittance?"

"That's right. And Dolly is no clean potato, let me tell you! She comes across as nice and everything like that, but she gets Boris to do all her dirty work."

"Yes, I have heard that," I said. "So, do you think Dolly and Boris would have been angry enough to murder Sheila McFeeler?"

Harriet narrowed her eyes. "Possibly. I certainly wouldn't discount them. And they would give each other an alibi, not that anyone needed an alibi because nobody knew when the brakes were cut. The murderer had all night to cut the brakes. It could have happened at any time."

"Yes, it *is* quite difficult," I said. "Can you think of any other suspects?"

She looked blank. "No, I can't."

"What about Walsh?" I asked her.

"Walsh? Why would he be a suspect?"

"Because he bought Dolly and Boris's café, and he would have done very well out of it if the coffee law had been overturned, and that was never going to happen so long as Sheila supported it."

Harriet nodded slowly. "Yes, there is that. But Walsh seems a lovely young man, not like Boris." Her nose wrinkled with distaste.

"What about Walsh's girlfriend, Madison?"

"Oh, does Walsh have a girlfriend? I didn't know that."

I exchanged glances with Oleander. Harriet certainly hadn't been any help. Sure, she also suspected Boris, but she hadn't come up with any new names. I tried one last time. "Is there anyone at the retirement home who knew Sheila McFeeler well? Or do you know anybody who had a reason to harm her?"

Harriet shook her head vigorously. "No one else. That's all the residents and I have been discussing ever since it happened. I mean, there is nothing else interesting on the news, is there? The only news we ever have here is of bushfires or floods, maybe viruses, but murder—that's something else again, isn't it!" Her face lit up and then fell with disappointment. "And cutting brake lines. How unimaginative. Now, if poison had been used…" Her voice trailed away, and a wistful look passed over her face. "That would have been more interesting. And maybe I could have procured a photo of her liver."

CHAPTER 13

Max hurried over to me as soon as I arrived at the funeral. "What are you doing here, Goldie?" he asked in a scolding tone. "You didn't know Sheila McFeeler."

"I did know her a bit," I said defensively, "but I know her son Tristan much better."

He put his hands on his hips. "Exactly how do you know Tristan?"

"I'm selling the house for him, once it's in his name."

Max looked as though he wanted to say more but hurried away when Detective Rick Power beckoned to him.

Oleander tugged on my arm. "That was a close call."

"We *do* have a legitimate reason for being here," I said, "but I was going to mention Harriet as well."

"He didn't give you the chance," Athanasius said. "Maybe, he will question you again, and you can say we're here to support Harriet."

Harriet looked quite pleased with herself. We had roped her into coming along. I was going to say we were there to support Harriet who was quite upset that Sheila had died. If Max had questioned her, she would have simply described diseases to him which would have made him lose interest in questioning her quite quickly. She was the ideal person to have with us as a cover for being at the funeral.

"Let's sit in the back row so we can observe everyone," Harriet said. She was clearly enjoying the murder investigation.

I sat next to her, but as soon as my bottom hit the seat, she grabbed my arm, her bony fingers digging into my wrist painfully. "Dolly and Boris Florette are here!" she hissed.

Oleander leant over me to speak to Harriet. "That's not suspicious. Lots of townspeople are here."

"I *do* think it is suspicious," Harriet whispered

back. "Doris and Boris hated Sheila. I'm sure they're only here at her funeral because they murdered her."

"How do you figure that?" I asked her.

"Murderers always attend the funerals of their victims," she said in a knowing way. "It's a well-known fact. That's why the police always attend the funerals." She nodded to Max and the other detectives, Rick Power and John Walters.

It only just then occurred to me that I hadn't seen the other two detectives around town, investigating this murder. Maybe, it was because I wasn't a suspect and hadn't discovered the body this time. That suited me just fine.

"Her son, Tristan Smith, is having her cremated," Harriet continued.

"How do you know that?" Athanasius asked in a booming voice.

People turned around to look at him.

"Keep your voice down," Oleander admonished him.

He nodded and then repeated, "How did you know that?" in hushed tones.

"Because everyone at the retirement home was talking about it," she said. "One of the ladies is the mother of the funeral director."

I nodded slowly. I would have to file that away for future reference. It could come in handy at some point.

"Did we ever find out why Sheila was driving to Brisbane that day?" I asked the others.

They all shook their heads. "Maybe I can ask Tristan later," I said. I looked for him, but he was sitting down the front row. He seemed genuinely upset. He certainly had a motive if what they said about his business was true, but then again, Max would know that and hadn't made an arrest. Or maybe he suspected Tristan and just didn't have the evidence yet. I wondered if I could find a way to get the information out of Max.

After a considerable time pondering the matter, I formulated a plan. The opportunity presented itself minutes later. Max walked to the back of the room alone, so I jumped from my seat and joined him. "Can I have a word with you outside?" I asked.

We walked out onto the porch.

"Do you think it's safe for me to have Tristan Smith as a client?" I asked him in my most feminine voice, batting my eyelids at him coquettishly.

"Is something wrong with your eyes, Goldie?" he asked with concern.

BROOM SERVICE

I shook my head. "No. Max, do you think I'm in any physical danger having Tristan Smith as a client?" I patted his arm seductively and leant into him.

He took me by both arms and steadied me. "Are you coming down with the flu? Do you have a middle ear infection? You just listed to one side."

I stomped my foot. "Max! You haven't answered my question. I'm scared, being a female living on her own with just a wombat for protection. Do you think I'm in any danger from Tristan Smith? I'm selling his mother's house for him, and so I'll be in close contact with him."

Max scratched his head. "Why would you be in danger from Tristan?"

"I mean, what if he's the killer? The house would be worth around six hundred thousand dollars, and word around town is that he's broke. If you suspected him, you would tell me, wouldn't you, Max? Then maybe, I could suggest another real estate agent for him."

Max shot me a long hard look. "You *are* investigating Sheila's murder, aren't you?"

I shook my head. "Oh, good gracious me, no! Whatever gives you that idea? I'm scared because you haven't found the killer yet. What if they come after me next?"

"Why would the murderer come after you? You had nothing to do with Sheila McFeeler."

I put my hands over my eyes and tried something else. "I can't help being scared, Max. What if Tristan murdered his mother and then decided to go on a killing spree?"

Max wagged his finger at me. "You can't fool me, Goldie. You're investigating. How many times have I asked you not to investigate? You could be putting yourself in danger! If the killer discovers that you're sticking your nose in where it's not wanted, then you *will* be in danger."

Detective Power appeared and beckoned Max inside. "It's about to begin," he said, after shooting a dirty look at me.

Max put his arm on the small of my back and guided me inside. I took the seat between Oleander and Harriet, while Max continued down the other side of the chapel with the two detectives.

The chapel was small and depressing. The interior walls were brick, and the carpet was faded green. Hard wooden pews lined each side of the centre aisle, which led to a stage covered by dark blue curtains. The coffin, a plain wooden one, was on a stand at the front, but it wasn't open. Next to it, was a stand with a big photo of Sheila.

A chill descended upon me as I looked around the room. Chances were that the murderer was in that room with us right then and there. Who could it be? Dolly and Boris? Walsh? Walsh's girlfriend, Madison? Tristan? Or maybe, it was someone else entirely. If it was a witch who had murdered Sheila then maybe the witch wasn't at the funeral.

The more I thought about it, the more I was sure that my conclusion was right. If a witch had murdered Sheila, then the witch was someone who didn't live in town on a permanent basis. Still, Madison and Tristan were in the room, and neither of them lived in town permanently. Of course, there was the other possibility, namely that it was someone I didn't currently suspect. Maybe, I didn't even know them.

The minister walked out and cleared his throat. "The family has asked me to conduct a non-denominational service," he said in a disapproving tone.

Oleander whispered in my ear, "I'm sure Sheila would have wanted a pagan burial."

"Obviously, her son didn't know that," I whispered back. "Maybe, he didn't know she was a witch."

Oleander shook her head vigorously. "Of course, he knew she was a witch. If he didn't before, he would have found out when he saw her altar."

"He might not have understood the full implications of that," I pointed out.

The minister presently handed over to Tristan, who spoke beautifully and at length about what a wonderful person his mother was, how he had never known his father, and how his mother had been adopted. He said he never knew his father as he had left the family when Tristan was just six weeks old. Sheila had been from foster home to foster home and had never found her biological parents. He said he didn't know any other relatives.

Harriet burst into a flood of tears. Everybody turned around to look at her. "That poor boy," she said through her sobs. "Think of his spleen! Spleens carry emotional traumas."

"Come on, Harriet, I'll get you a drink of water," Oleander whispered. She helped Harriet out the back door.

I thought about what Tristan had said. It

certainly seemed genuine. Maybe, he wasn't the killer after all, but then again, I was fairly gullible and always thought the best of people.

I looked across at Walsh. I could only see the side of his face, but he certainly wasn't pretending to be upset. From the body language of Dolly and Boris, they were not pretending to be upset either. Boris had his arms crossed over his chest the whole time, and I couldn't see his face, but his shoulders were certainly rigid.

The minister made a speech about family members always being there for each other, which I thought was rather tactless, considering that Tristan was now left all alone in the world. When the minister stopped speaking, Tristan stood up once more. "Walsh has kindly offered his café. It's free cups of tea for everyone," he said. "We will all go there for the wake."

Some sad music played, and Tristan walked out the back of the room followed by people from the front rows.

"Shouldn't he have asked if anyone else wanted to say some words about Sheila?" I whispered to Athanasius.

Athanasius chuckled. "That would normally be the case at a funeral, but I'm sure Tristan was under no illusions as to how the whole town felt about Sheila. She was the only one on the Town Council who wanted to keep the old coffee bylaw, and although the other counsellors are here, I don't think any of them liked her." He nodded to the town counsellors who were walking past us.

"Then let's head off to Walsh's café," I said. "We can drink tea and question the suspects. Walsh can hardly slip us some coffee with all the cops around."

Harriet drove us all to Walsh's café in the retirement home bus. She had stopped sobbing, much to my relief.

When we arrived at the café, I saw Tristan speaking to some locals. I waited until they had left, and then I hurried over to him. "I'm sorry about your mother," I said. "I liked her. She seemed a nice person."

"Thank you," he said. "You're the first person who said she was nice."

"Well, I didn't agree with her supporting the old anti-coffee bylaw, but that doesn't mean I didn't like her," I said. "Tristan, I was meaning to ask you, did you know why your mother was driving to Brisbane that day?"

He looked blank. "What day?"

"The day that she was killed."

He ran his left hand through his hair. "Yes, I did. Gosh, it's been such a stressful day. Yes, the police asked me that too."

"Well, why did she drive to Brisbane?" I asked him.

"Apparently, she had a meeting with a lawyer," he said. "One of those hotshot Brisbane lawyers."

"How did you find that out?" I asked, trying not to sound too interested.

"It was on her iPad in her appointments," he said. "The police asked me if Mum kept her appointments in a book or on her computer, so I looked everywhere, and I found it on her iPad. They took the iPad, but then they gave it back."

"I see," I said, injecting a tone of nonchalance into my voice. "It must have been one of those lawyers who knew about overturning laws."

He nodded. "I thought so too."

"I hope it doesn't upset you to say this, but whoever cut your mother's brake lines must have known she was driving to Brisbane that day."

Tristan's brow furrowed. "I don't see the connection."

"Because if somebody cut her brake lines and

then she just drove around town that day, it would not have done any harm."

He continued to frown, processing what I said. Finally, recognition dawned on his face. "I see! Oh well, I guess you're right! Should I tell the police?"

I shook my head. "I'm sure they've already figured that out for themselves. That's why they wanted to know about her appointments. The thing is, Tristan, the murderer must have known your mother was driving to Brisbane that day, and that fact would surely eliminate some suspects."

"*I* knew she was driving to Brisbane that day," said a male voice from behind me.

I spun around. It was Walsh. "You did?" I said in shock.

He nodded and then his hand flew to his mouth. "I hope that doesn't make me a suspect?"

"How did you know?" Tristan asked him.

"Because your mother told us all. I said I was going to get a lawyer and she said she was getting a better lawyer, that Myles Pembroke guy who's always on TV. He's always trying to get high profile cases. He is a media whore. Anyway, she was gloating to us all about it."

"Who is *us all*?" I asked him.

"The whole Town Council," he said. "And she

was telling us in my café the day before she died. Sheila was having a loud argument with a woman. I had to intervene. She said she was sorry about the café, but she wanted to tell us that she was confident that Pembroke would somehow find a way to prevent us overturning the law. She said she was going to Brisbane the following day for a meeting with him."

"I wonder if the woman Sheila argued with was the murderer?" I said.

Tristan shook his head. "No, she actually fell over outside just after the argument when she was crossing the road in the storm. She broke her ankle and spent the following day in hospital."

"Do you remember who was in the café at that time?" I asked him. "Was anyone close enough to overhear?"

"I don't know, because there was that terrible storm at the time. It wasn't forecast, and it just came out of nowhere. Isn't the weather doing strange things lately! Anyway, I'll ask Madison later. She might remember." With that, he patted Tristan on the shoulder and walked away.

I wondered what to say to Tristan, but I needn't have worried, because a woman enveloped him in a big hug.

I hurried back to Oleander and relayed everything that had been said. "Then it *was* a sea witch," she said. "So, there was a terrible thunderstorm that came out of nowhere just as Sheila said she was going to drive to Brisbane the next day."

"But I assume Sheila was the one who caused the storm," I said. "She must have been upset."

Oleander shook her head. "But that's my point, Goldie, don't you see? Somebody, an evil witch, saw a storm come up suddenly. That means the witch must have realised at that very moment that Sheila was a sea witch. And as you know, sea witches are historically linked with East Bucklebury. If someone is looking to take a sea witch's powers, then they would come here looking for a sea witch."

"So, you think Sheila was just in the wrong place at the wrong time?" I asked her.

She nodded. "That's the way it's looking to me."

"It still could have been a coincidence," Athanasius said. "Just because Sheila McFeeler showed her sea witch abilities the day before she died doesn't mean another witch killed her. It still could be over the coffee law."

I agreed. "True. Anyway, there's something

else that has been puzzling me. Why is Tristan so friendly with Walsh? I mean, Tristan's mother and Walsh were on opposing sides."

"Maybe, they were in it together," Oleander said. "We'll have to find out why they are so friendly."

"You'll have to find out why who is so friendly?" Max said from behind us.

We both gasped and spun around. I'm sure we looked like kangaroos caught in the headlights.

"Just girl talk, if you must know, Max," Oleander said. "I was asking for Goldie's help with a man problem."

"Oh." Max frowned and walked away to mingle.

I turned to Oleander. "That was quick thinking."

"Am I your man problem?" Athanasius asked her. "What did I do wrong?"

Oleander rolled her eyes. "You didn't do anything wrong. We were lying to Max. He thought he'd caught us investigating again."

Harriet was stuffing her face full of cakes. I walked over to her and waited until she had finished one. "Do you know why Walsh let Tristan have the wake in his café?" I asked her.

She shrugged. "I don't have a clue. I only moved to town not all that long ago, if you'll recall. Still, I could ask around the retirement home, if you like."

"That would be good," I said. "If you find out, could you tell Oleander or Athanasius?"

"I sure will." She stuffed a peppermint chocolate cupcake into her mouth.

"I think I'll go home now," I said to Oleander.

She wrinkled her nose. "How will you get home? I don't think it's safe for you to walk home with a murderer on the loose."

"I'll take you," Max said, appearing beside me once more.

I turned back to Oleander. "Max will take me home."

"Not home," Max said. "We're going to do a fun thing with my parents and my stepmother."

CHAPTER 14

a fun thing with Max's family? I liked Jack and Delilah, but Tabitha? Not in the slightest. She was a spawn of hell, as far as I was concerned.

And so, less than half an hour later, I found myself sitting on the beach with Jack, Delilah, and the dreaded Tabitha. I had not been able to bring Persnickle. "Tabitha, is your favourite colour orange?" I asked her.

"Of course," she snapped. "I thought that would have been entirely obvious to anyone, even to someone of your low intelligence."

Delilah looked shocked, but Jack's expression didn't change. He continued to stare out to sea.

"I prefer beaches with waves," Tabitha said in

a whiny tone. "How anyone can live in a stupid, little town on the broadwater is quite beyond me. Still, I suppose it's useful in tsunamis because the tsunami would hit the outlying islands first."

Jack scratched his head. "I don't know if that science holds up," he said, "but I'm not a meteorologist or a geologist or whoever knows about those things."

Tabitha pursed her lips, or to be accurate, did the best impression she could, considering her face had probably been lifted more than five hundred times. "No, you're not."

"Well then, I'll have to agree with whatever you say," Jack said with a chuckle.

I could see Delilah looked decidedly put out, and I wondered if she still had a thing for Jack. I had no idea why he preferred the horrible Tabitha to the entirely pleasant Delilah, although I supposed love can't be understood at the best of times. I scratched my head.

Tabitha was wearing a bright orange dress with the kind of geometric pattern that reminded me of the 1980s bathrooms I'd seen many a time in my real estate career. It matched her bright orange hair. I would just have to keep Persnickle away from her—there was nothing else for it.

I forced a smile. "So, how long can you stay?"

"Are you hoping we'll leave soon?" Tabitha said angrily.

"Goldie was just being polite," Delilah said. Her face flushed red.

Tabitha lifted her face and jutted out her chin. "Whatever. Max, did you bring wine?"

"I bought bubbly," Max said. "It's not every day I get to spend time with my family, and the funeral took a few hours."

"But you were working at the funeral, weren't you!" his father said astutely. "That was work, not a social thing for you."

"I knew the victim, so I had to go anyway," Max said.

Tabitha continued to purse her lips. "I thought you would have solved the murder by now," she said with malice in her tone. "A clever boy like you—or so your father says—and you haven't even figured out who did it yet."

Delilah looked at Jack, no doubt expecting him to say something, but he simply looked down at his knees. We were sitting on a picnic rug, all in a circle. It would have been good if we were performing a ritual, but then I was the only witch there, as far as I knew anyway. I chuckled to myself.

I looked up to see Delilah's face was still bright red.

"My son is a very good detective, and I'm sure he already has a suspect."

"I'm sure he doesn't," Tabitha countered.

I looked at Max, hoping the exchange would somehow encourage him to divulge some information.

"I can't discuss police matters," was all he said.

"What a shame you became a detective and didn't follow in your father's footsteps to become a very wealthy businessman," Tabitha said.

Delilah looked as though she was about to explode, so I quickly said, "Bubbly, anyone? Max, let's all have some now."

Max opened the picnic basket and produced a blue wine glass for everyone. He hurried to fill the glasses with bubbly.

"I don't like to drink on an empty stomach," Delilah said, and would have said more, but Tabitha interrupted her.

"You could have fooled me," she said in a stage whisper.

I wondered if there was going to be an

outright fight, so I asked, "What delicious food do you have for us, Max?"

"I have lovely crusty French bread rolls." He wasted no time producing one from the hamper.

"And I have some dairy-free margarine."

Tabitha made a strangled sound, and I thought she was having some sort of an attack, but she said, "Dairy-free margarine! Whatever will they think of next? My, we have got fancy in this funny little town."

I wondered if she could be more obnoxious if she tried. I wondered what Jack saw in her. They obviously didn't share a love for the colour orange, so what else could it be? It certainly wasn't her personality. Maybe, his business had been going under, and he had to marry a wealthy woman. I nodded to myself. Yes, that must be it. I couldn't see any other reason he would have married her.

Something occurred to me. Maybe, she was blackmailing him. Yes, that had to be it. She had some dirt on him. I had no idea what it could be. I bit my lip and thought about it, until I realised Max was speaking to me.

"Goldie? Earth to Goldie? You were a million miles away."

"I was just thinking about blackmail," I said, and I clamped my hand over my mouth.

"Honestly, Goldie, I told you not to investigate the case."

"Actually, it was nothing to do with Sheila McFeeler," I said, hoping he wouldn't press me.

Fortunately for me, he didn't. He laid out some platters in the middle of the blanket and heaped piles of delicious food on top of it. We all ate in silence. I would have said it was a companionable silence, and it would have been, apart from the fact that Tabitha was there.

Jack was the first to speak. "It's a shame you haven't solved the case, Max, because then we could spend more time together. We haven't seen much of you."

"Surely, you must suspect who did it?" Tabitha asked. "You must have some suspects. What about the victim's son?"

"How did you know she had a son?" I asked her.

"It's all over town," she said. "It's all the poor son this, the poor son that. I've been all over town looking for coffee, and no one will serve me any. I do hope you have some in that picnic basket, Max."

"Yes, but please don't let anyone know I have it," he said. "It would go very badly for me if anyone found out that I had coffee. I'm sure Detective Power wouldn't mind me going down."

"Such a stupid law," Tabitha said. "No wonder that woman was murdered."

"Tabitha!" Jack said in shock.

"I didn't say I was glad she was dead," she said in a scolding tone. "I just said it was no wonder she was murdered, and that's a fact. All these poor coffee deprived people in that town." She waved her hand expansively in the direction of town. "They have to go without coffee. That selfish woman opposed coffee purely for commercial reasons to get her tearoom going. Surely, you don't have to look far to find the murderer, Max! If I was a betting woman, I would say the murderer was right under your nose!"

Max looked decidedly uncomfortable. "I can't discuss police business," he said.

From his tone, I realised that he really didn't have a clue.

That concerned me. More and more, I was thinking the murder wasn't a mundane one. If it had been, I was certain Max would have been on top of it and would have solved it by now. I had come to know Max fairly well, and I didn't get the impression he had any clue as to the identity of the murderer. It had to be witch.

The only clue I had to the murderer was that it wasn't a permanent resident. Walsh was a permanent resident, but his girlfriend wasn't. The victim's son, Tristan Smith, wasn't a permanent resident. Tristan obviously knew where Sheila lived, and it would have been easy for Walsh's girlfriend to find out. And then, of course, there was Dolly, and her husband, Boris. They certainly had a serious grudge against Sheila, and everybody said that Boris had a terrible temper. What's more, he had been a mechanic, and although anybody could easily find out how to cut brake lines, it seemed to be the type of murder that a mechanic would commit. I was certain that if I was both a mechanic and a murderer, I would murder somebody by doing something to their car.

I didn't know whether I should say anything to Max, but finally, I said, "I think the townspeople suspect Boris Florette."

Max looked surprised. "Is that what they're saying?"

I nodded. "And that's what they think at the retirement home, too. They say that Boris has a terrible temper. In fact, he was a client of Harriet's some time ago, and while she couldn't divulge any patient information, she did say that he had a terrible temper."

Tabitha leant forward. "But did he have a motive? You do need a motive to kill somebody, I hope you realise. Otherwise, there would be a lot more dead people in the world, if people with terrible tempers just murdered people willy-nilly."

I shot her my best glare.

Max looked exasperated with her, but before he could say anything, I said, "Yes, he had a motive all right. He and his wife had a café and it wasn't doing well. They thought they could trade out of it, until Sheila decided to open a tearoom and support the anti-coffee law. They then had to sell the business to a song for Walsh."

"Then it must be Boris," Tabitha said. "That should be obvious even to you, Max. He did it, either acting alone or with his wife."

Max took a deep breath and let it out slowly, and then rubbed his temples. I felt sorry for him having such a stepmother. She really was a wicked stepmother just like the ones in fairy tales.

"Thanks for all that, Tabitha," he said in a tone that didn't sound thankful at all.

Delilah cleared her throat. "Do we have cake?"

Max smiled with relief. "We sure do." He reached into the hamper and produced a huge lemon meringue pie and a cake knife.

I clasped my hands with delight. "I love lemon meringue pie."

I had only eaten one mouthful when Max got a call. He looked at the caller ID before jumping to his feet and walking over to this car.

He came back, his face grim.

CHAPTER 15

"What has happened, Max?" I asked with concern.

"I'm afraid I can't tell you—it's police business," he said, "but I have to go."

I looked at Tabitha. "I have to go too, because the protest rally is starting soon."

I hadn't really wanted to go to the protest rally. I had intended to put in an appearance, but it was either the protest rally or putting up with Tabitha, so the protest rally won hands down.

"You need to stay here and entertain us," Tabitha said with pursed lips.

"I'm sorry, but I'm going to have to cut this short," Max said. "Goldie, I'll take you home, and then I'll drive Mum and Dad and Tabitha to their motels."

We packed up the picnic stuff, Tabitha complaining all the while. "Honestly, I was enjoying that," she said. "We should have waited here, and Goldie could have driven back with her car." Tabitha shot me a mean look.

"As a real estate agent, I really do have to attend the rally," I lied.

When Max dropped me back at my house, I hurried inside as fast as I could. Once safely inside, I looked out the living room windows. Max's car wasn't there and thankfully, neither was Tabitha. That woman was certainly something else!

I changed my clothes and put on some sensible shoes. The rally was in the local park, and I figured I might be sloshing through mud. Persnickle opened one eye and then promptly went back to sleep.

Soon, I was on my way to the rally. I hadn't even bothered to check the time, and so I was surprised when I got there early. Walsh was standing on a crate addressing the small crowd. "Madison has invited the press, so let's be on our best behaviour. Espresso your opinions politely."

I groaned, but everyone else laughed. I certainly hoped he wouldn't make any more coffee puns. The crowd presently dispersed. Walsh stationed someone at the entrance at the park to hand out leaflets while the others held up placards. I tried to make myself as invisible as I could by hiding behind a huge jacaranda tree. I certainly didn't want to be arrested, and I wouldn't have been surprised if there was an old bylaw that stated it was illegal for more than five people to gather in a public place. Nothing would surprise me about the old East Bucklebury laws.

I heard chanting, so I peeked out from behind the tree. Walsh and the others were stomping around in a circle, chanting "Make coffee legal; make coffee legal."

It was the most unimaginative chant, but then again, I supposed it made their aim perfectly clear. I saw a photographer setting up a camera on a tripod. The protestors continued to stomp around in a circle. Their chanting grew louder and louder by the minute. I noticed Madison was standing off to one side and not joining in. I assumed she was there to wrangle the media.

I put my head down and skirted around the park, intending to come up behind her. I waited for a moment behind each tree, so it took me a while to reach her. Finally, I came up behind her, right beside the public fountain. She was talking to a man with a camera from one of the big Brisbane television stations. He was loudly expressing surprise about the bylaw.

While they were chatting, Detective Power arrived on the scene. "I'm going to arrest you all," he said in a booming voice. "This is an illegal protest."

I popped back behind the nearest tree.

From my vantage point, I could still hear Madison. "The journalists here will find that very interesting," she said. "They are already interested in the antiquated bylaw. I'm sure if you arrest the protestors, they will become martyrs, and it will attract national if not international attention."

I could see Detective Power's face. Even from the distance, I could see he was angry. After a moment, he stomped back to his police car, but instead of driving away, just sat in it. All of a sudden, there was a crack of thunder and a heavy storm came up from nowhere. Even though I was under a spreading tibouchina tree, I was drenched right through to the bone.

There hadn't been any clouds a minute earlier.

This had to be the work of a sea witch. But was the rally the target? It made no sense. Surely, the murderer didn't have a problem with the anti-coffee protesters, especially after murdering Sheila who was a supporter of the anti-coffee law. I shook my head, sending droplets of rain flying. No, that didn't make any sense at all.

The sound of the rain obliterated Madison's words, leaving me only aware of my own thoughts. Why would the sea witch make it rain heavily on the protestors? Or could there be another target? I didn't think anything else was going on in town at the time. The only other possibility I could think of was that the sea witch was currently having an argument with someone. I thought about it some more, and figured I was right—the murderer was either in a terrible mood or had specifically targeted the protest rally.

I sprinted for my car. I had to run right past the police vehicle, and I saw Detective Power staring at me as I went. Just as I reached my car, a hand clamped down on my arm. I spun around. It was Walsh.

"Thanks so much for coming today, Goldie. It seems the weather wasn't on our side."

I wiped the rain out of my eyes. "That's for sure!"

"We're going to meet back at my café now. The journalists are going to interview me there."

"That's a good idea," I said.

"We're heading there right now."

I nodded and got in my car. Obviously, Walsh had not seen me hiding behind a tree and thought I had been involved in the protest rally. Maybe, it was a good thing we were meeting back at the café, because I would be able to question the suspects.

I drove home to change out of my wet clothes. By the time I got to Walsh's café, most of the others were there and they were still dripping wet. The rain had just stopped, and the sun was now out.

"Do you often get these freak storms?" the journalist standing near the front door asked Madison.

She shook her head. "No, although there have been one or two recently."

I walked along the tables, looking for suspects. I saw Tristan sitting by himself. "Mind if I join you?" I asked him.

"Certainly." He gestured to a chair. "All these people seem to have been caught in a storm."

"There was a protest rally against the anti-coffee law," I told him.

He nodded. "I figured as much. You didn't go?"

"I didn't take part, but I went for a look. I went home and changed before I came here," I told him.

"Have you heard? The police have taken somebody in for questioning."

I sat on the edge of my seat. "Who was that?"

"Boris Florette."

"Boris!" I repeated in a shrill voice. "Have they arrested him?"

Tristan shrugged. "I don't know. I heard people saying he had been taken in for questioning because he threatened my mother."

"She didn't tell me that!" I realised what I'd said and silently rebuked myself. I hurried to add, "Not that I knew her that well, of course." *I didn't know her at all when she was alive*, I added silently.

Tristan did not seem to notice anything amiss. "Yes, apparently he yelled at her in the street in front of witnesses. He said she'd sent him broke and said he wished she would drop dead."

"A lot of people say things like that..." I began, but Tristan interrupted me.

"The police are taking it seriously, obviously."

I nodded. That must have been the call Max had received.

A woman sitting at the table directly behind me cleared her throat loudly. "I couldn't help hearing what you two said," she said.

I swung around. She pushed on. "I was one of the people who overheard Boris say that to Sheila. He was yelling at her. I was quite scared, to tell you the truth. He said he and his wife had worked hard all their lives and now they had nothing to show for it, because she was supporting the anti-coffee law."

"But that's not logical," I protested. "That law has been around for decades."

The woman shook her head. "But there was the public perception that Walsh might have been able to get it overturned. Once Sheila came back to town and started spouting that she would support it no matter what, well, that really put paid to Dolly and Boris selling the café for decent money."

Tristan nodded slowly. "You know, I wonder if Walsh and Mum were in it together."

I was shocked by his words. "Whatever do you mean?"

"Walsh bought this café for a song. My mother supporting the anti-coffee law certainly helped Walsh financially."

I thought about what he said. That certainly did make sense, but even if that were the case, would Walsh have had a motive to murder Sheila?

CHAPTER 16

"I'm still not sure it was Boris," I said to Oleander. We were sitting in my living room, drinking coffee. "This investigation is going nowhere. It even seems Max is stumped."

"Has he said anything?" Oleander asked me.

I shook my head. "No, you know Max. Still, I can sense he's frustrated, and it's not just because Tabitha is visiting."

Oleander agreed. "I'm sure he would have liked a nice visit from his parents without Tabitha."

I nodded. "She really is the evil stepmother of fairytale proportions," I said. "What Jack sees in her is beyond me."

"Maybe you should take Persnickle back to speak with Sheila."

"I was thinking about that," I said. "With Tristan staying in Sheila's house, we obviously can't go back there—not to the house itself I mean, but we could park outside."

"Tristan will notice if you park outside," Oleander protested. "It's the only house at that end of the street."

"Yes, I know that, but I thought we could drive past and park in the mangroves like we did the other day."

Soon, Oleander, Athanasius, Persnickle, and I were heading for Sheila's side of town. I didn't know if it was going to work, but what did I have to lose? Besides, I was becoming more aware of a witchy presence in town. It felt malevolent. As yet, it didn't seem focused on me, but I didn't want to take any chances.

"Don't turn in there!" Athanasius shrieked. "You'll get bogged."

"We parked there before," Oleander told him.

I myself didn't like the look of the ground. "It's rained since we were last here," I said. "I won't go in too far. This should be fine. I can't see the house from here."

I rolled down my window and a huge mosquito flew in.

"Roll that window up now!" Oleander exclaimed. "That mosquito's the size of a horse!"

I rolled my window up and yelled, "Sheila! Sheila McFeeler, are you here?" I called for some time, but she didn't respond.

"Maybe, you and Persnickle should get out of the car," Athanasius suggested. "I have some mosquito repellent in my pocket."

I turned around and looked over the back seat. Athanasius pulled a bottle out of his pocket, but Persnickle lunged for it. Athanasius snatched it away from Persnickle in the nick of time. "He thought it was a lemon tart," Athanasius said, producing a lemon tart from his other pocket and feeding it to Persnickle, who ate it with a satisfied grunt.

Athanasius handed the insect repellent to me. "Don't put it on until you get outside the car," he cautioned. "It smells foul."

I got out of the car and sprayed myself with the repellent. Persnickle shot me a puzzled look. "You don't need any. You have natural wombat protection," I told him. I was about to call out for Sheila when she materialised in front of me. I gasped. "Sheila!" I said in surprise.

"You called?" she said dryly.

"The police have taken Boris Florette in for questioning," I told her. "Why didn't you tell me he threatened you?"

She scratched her head. "He threatened me? Is that what they're saying?"

I nodded. "He apparently threatened you in front of a bunch of witnesses. He said he wished you were dead."

Sheila looked puzzled. "And the cops took him in for questioning over that? He's been saying he wanted me dead for ages. He didn't actually say he was going to kill me."

"Well, the police must have thought there was a good reason to take him in," I countered. "Do you think he might have killed you?"

"Anything's possible." She floated upwards a little before floating back down to the ground. "Somebody did it, and it's obviously someone I don't suspect, so it could be anybody." She threw up her hands to the sky.

"Did you sense any malice from Boris towards you?"

Sheila chuckled. "Of course, I did! He hated

me, that's for sure, but as for killing me? I don't know if he had it in him."

"What about his wife, Dolly?"

Sheila waved her finger at me. "If it had to be one of them, I would definitely think it was Dolly rather than Boris. She seems nice and pleasant to everybody, but she's a nasty schemer, that one. Boris wears his heart on his sleeve and says exactly what's on his mind, whereas she's duplicitous and scheming."

"Do you think she would have it in her to murder somebody?"

Sheila's answer came swiftly. "Not really, but like I said, *someone* murdered me. I've had nothing to do but think about it, and I haven't come up with one particular person. It could have been Dolly, or it could have been Boris."

"Or Walsh?"

She nodded. "Or Walsh. He certainly saw me as someone standing in his way."

"Have you thought of anything else since we last spoke?" I asked her.

"I'm surprised the police haven't arrested somebody by now. Goldie, do you think it could have been a witch?"

"I don't want to think so, but I must admit, it's

looking that way. There was a protest rally against the anti-coffee bylaw at the park yesterday, and there was a sudden storm. I was certain it was the work of a sea witch."

Sheila agreed. "Yes, that did not feel like a natural storm to me at all, that's for sure. So, if it's a witch passing through town, how did they know I was a sea witch?"

"Didn't you cause a sudden storm when you were in Walsh's café the day before you were murdered?"

"Yes, and the sky was perfectly blue and clear, and the humidity was low, so everybody did think that the storm was strange. If a witch looking for a sea witch was in the café at the time, then I would have been the prime suspect because I was the one who was angry."

"And Walsh's girlfriend, Madison, was there at the time. Do you remember who else was there?"

She shook her head. "I vaguely remember there were plenty of tourists, people I hadn't seen before. Goldie, watch your back, or you'll end up like me. I think somebody has come to this town looking for sea witches."

A cold chill ran up my spine. "What makes you say that?"

"Because it would be too much of a coincidence for a bad witch to be in the café right when I caused the storm, unless that witch had been hunting sea witches. And only witches, or people who knew about sea witches, would have known I inadvertently caused that storm. Besides, East Bucklebury is well known in certain circles for attracting sea witches. It's lucky that witches who hunt sea witches are few and far between, or you'd be dead right now."

"Thanks a lot," I said dryly. "So as it stands, you think a witch was the culprit?"

"I do. I've given it a lot of thought. After all, what else is there to do? I can't watch Netflix. I've definitely given it a lot of thought, and I think it was a witch. And if you weren't responsible for the storm yesterday, then surely it was the murderer."

"But there could be another sea witch in town, and we wouldn't know it," I said. "I mean, an innocent sea witch. You didn't know I was a sea witch, and I didn't know you were one, and we were both living in the same town."

"I take your point," she said, "but I can feel something building up. There's something around making me uneasy, and I'm sure it's the witch who killed me. You have to be very careful, or you might be next." With that, she vanished.

I slapped away a few mosquitoes, which apparently liked the taste of the mosquito repellent, and put Persnickle back in the car. He stuck his nose in Athanasius's pocket, so Athanasius promptly produced another lemon tart. While Persnickle gobbled it up, I relayed the conversation to Athanasius and Oleander.

"And how on earth are we going to track down an evil witch who hunts sea witches?" I concluded.

"I think we need to go back to the retirement home and question Betty," Oleander said. "She's the mother of the funeral director. She might have some information on Tristan Smith."

I took her meaning at once. "So, you're thinking Tristan could be the witch?" I asked her.

Oleander nodded. "He *is* one of our three witch possibilities, remember?"

Athanasius agreed. "Tristan, Madison, and 'unknown witch.'"

To my relief, I was able to reverse the car without spinning the wheels at all. If there had been any more rain, the car would have been bogged for sure, so I made a mental note never to park there again.

When we reached the retirement home, the man at the gate waved us through. We waved to him and proceeded. As soon as I got out of the car, I put on Persnickle's leash and his wombat therapy blanket.

"We're in luck." Oleander pointed to a woman sitting at a table under a big blue beach umbrella. "That's Betty there, and she's sitting alone."

I remembered Betty from my previous visits. She was ninety-two, and a highly skilled in knitting and crochet. Her fingers were always working away at her knitting.

We walked over and sat next to her. "You've come to question me about Tristan Smith," she said. Her tone held no hint of question, only fact.

We all nodded. "If that's all right?" I asked her.

She knitted away without looking down at her hands. "That's fine. I've been expecting you. I was bored sitting alone, and the others are helping with room service. I don't know much about Tristan Smith, only that he now has no relatives. He and his mother weren't estranged by any means, but they weren't on the best of terms. My daughter tells me that Tristan chose the cheapest option for everything for his mother's funeral and service."

"Is that because he was broke, or because he didn't like his mother?" I asked her.

She had come to the end of the row, so she flipped her knitting needles over and started on the next row. "My daughter said it could have been a little bit of both. He spoke well of his mother, but he told my daughter he had been living at Mermaid Waters for some time and hadn't visited her in ages. He used to be a wealthy businessman, but he lost all his money, and he thought his mother would be ashamed of him."

"So it might not have been that he disliked his mother; he was afraid of what she would think," I said.

Betty agreed. "That's the way I interpreted it. Anyway, my daughter said he chose the cheapest option for everything. He didn't seem to have much money at all, and he had to approach his mother's bank to give him the money for the funeral expenses from Sheila's account."

"So, maybe he did murder his mother for money, after all," Athanasius said.

I expected Betty to be shocked by his words, but her expression remained impassive. "Quite possibly. My daughter had to tell him how to get the money for the funeral expenses. She told him that if Sheila had less than ten thousand dollars in her bank account, then the bank would release that money to him, as he was the executor."

"And I'm guessing Sheila did have less than ten thousand dollars in her bank account?" I asked.

Betty nodded. "Yes, she had just under seven thousand dollars in her account. The bank wrote the cheque for Sheila's funeral expenses."

"But I thought you said the bank would release all the money to Tristan?" Athanasius said.

Betty shook her head and then nodded, knitting all the while. "Yes, technically they do, but it could take a few weeks. He has to give them the death certificate, which my daughter applied for on his behalf. Of course, Tristan could have applied for the death certificate himself, but he would have had to pay for it, whereas because my daughter applied for it, the bank wrote the cheque for that as well."

I spotted some flowers and tightened my grip on Persnickle's leash. "There's a lot to it all, that's for sure. Did your daughter happen to mention whether she thought Tristan might have murdered his mother?"

For the first time, Betty showed surprise. "She didn't actually say," she said, "and my daughter is usually forthright in giving her opinion, so I doubt she did think that. She only told me that Tristan was obviously broke, and he was highly worried about money."

Athanasius, Oleander, and I exchanged glances. "Thanks, you've been very helpful," Oleander said. "Goldie, we'll walk you to your car."

As soon as we were out of earshot, Oleander turned to me. "That was useful as far as finding out Tristan is broke. That gives him a motive for murder, but we're no closer to discovering whether he's a witch."

"That sudden storm at the protest rally was definitely caused by a sea witch," I told them. "It had magic stamped all over it. Still, I have no idea of the reason behind it." I planted my palm on my forehead. "I should have asked Sheila whether anyone else was in support of the anti-coffee laws."

"You didn't need to ask Sheila that," Oleander said. "Anybody in town could tell you that. You could simply ask Walsh, but I suspect that there were no other supporters, or we would have heard of it by now."

"You're right. But where do we go from here?"

I was met with blank faces. None of us had a clue. Just then, there was a loud crack of thunder and black clouds rolled in. "It's the sea witch again," I said. "Whoever it is, is closing in."

CHAPTER 17

I parked my car in the retirement village outside Oleander's apartment. This case was confusing me, and I needed a little help from my friends. I knocked several times on Oleander's door. There was no response, so I walked to the main complex. I was surprised that I didn't come across any residents on the way.

The reception desk was empty, so I headed down to Athanasius's door. He wasn't there, either. It seemed the whole place was deserted.

I turned around to see Harriet hurrying the other way. I called after her. "Harriet, hi. I'm just looking for…"

"I wouldn't know anything about that," Harriet replied over her shoulder.

That was strange. Harriet usually wanted to show me her ghastly book. Something didn't feel right, and where were Oleander and Athanasius? I hadn't called ahead, sure, but it's not like the pair had many hobbies besides sleuthing. Surely, they were just as keen as I was to solve this case? Or maybe not.

It wasn't just Oleander and Athanasius who had vanished off the face of the earth. It was everyone. I hurried after Harriet.

"It has nothing to do with me," Harriet said when I caught her, "which is why I'm not going to tell you to check the mangrove swamp." She walked into a room and locked the door behind her.

I scratched my head. The mangrove swamp? Now why on earth would the residents and the staff of the retirement home be in the mangrove swamp?

I walked back outside and headed straight for the mangroves that formed the back border to the property. It wasn't long before I was treading through their slippery branches, rain splashing the exposed skin on my face and hands. I looked down to see at least five mosquitos on my arm. I swiped at them with a grunt.

I was going to kill Oleander and Athanasius. Who runs off into a swamp without so much as leaving a note? And precisely where in the mangrove swamp could they be? And what were they doing? Surely, it had to be something illegal. My stomach sank.

I didn't have to wait long for answers. Soon, I found myself staring at a small encampment. The encampment was hung with camouflage netting. I would have walked straight past it if not for the armed guards standing at the entrance. It seemed the guards were over ninety years old and armed with bright yellow water pistols.

What on earth was happening here? Instead of walking up to the guards and asking them, I slipped around to the side and decided to crawl under the camouflage netting. I was already covered with mosquitoes, so a little mud was not going to bother me.

To my surprise, the camouflage netting was hiding an old building that looked well over a century old. But I didn't have time to study the architecture. The residents of the retirement village were working at tables scattered around the room. At first, I couldn't see what they were working on, but then I crept a little closer. Coffee beans! The retirement village residents were scooping coffee beans out of huge hessian bags and repackaging them into smaller paper bags.

"Goldie?"

"Oleander?"

Oleander was at the nearest table with a silver scoop in her hand. "I had no idea you were coming, Goldie!"

Athanasius poked his head around the camouflage netting before strolling into the room. "Goldie, you could have called ahead."

I put my hands on my hips. "What is going on? You're packing coffee beans in a mangrove swamp."

Oleander and Athanasius exchanged sheepish glances. "Well…" Athanasius began, but Oleander interrupted him.

"The residents run a coffee smuggling operation," Oleander admitted. "It's called Operation Room Service."

I could not believe what I was hearing. "Surely, you're not serious?" When they didn't respond, I added, "Why on earth didn't you tell me?"

Oleander looked guilty. "We couldn't tell you because of Max. We didn't want to put you in an awkward situation. Besides, Athanasius and I rarely help."

Everyone had stopped packing the coffee beans and now they were all staring at me. "What's with the guards outside?" I asked.

Oleander shrugged. "They are just to deter people. The guns are actually water pistols."

"I figured that. So, why are you packing coffee in a mangrove swamp? Coffee is illegal in East Bucklebury, as you well know."

Athanasius nodded. "That's precisely why we are packing coffee in a mangrove swamp. We couldn't possibly run this operation in the middle of town now, could we? And this is the shipment that's going out to Walsh. He's our best customer."

"How has this been happening under my nose this whole time?"

Oleander chuckled. "You've been a little distracted by all the murders. Also, by the man whose job it is to solve murders. Coffee?" she added.

I sighed. "Fine." I couldn't stand the gorgeous smell of coffee without drinking any, so five minutes later, I found myself back in the retirement home's lounge, drinking a latte.

"How did the residents even think of this operation?" I said as I set down my mug.

"A few of the residents have connections in Hawaii, where we source our beans. It's not actually that difficult to establish an illicit smuggling operation," Oleander said.

I shook my head. "No, not that. You know you can easily buy coffee from anywhere outside East Bucklebury?" I put my head in my hands.

"The residents needed an activity," Oleander said. "The illegal coffee smuggling operation keeps them happy. Besides, their favourite show on Netflix is *Narcos*."

I groaned. "This is terrible."

"I can make it again?"

"Not the coffee. This is the best coffee I have ever tasted. What am I going to tell Max?"

"Nothing. Just keep it our secret for now," Athanasius replied.

I did not like lying to Max, but how could I betray my friends? Besides, it would put Max in an uncomfortable position. Yes, the best thing for now was to keep this whole thing to myself. One day, I had to tell Max I was a sea witch, but for now, this was also a secret I had to keep to myself.

And no more visits to any more mangrove swamps. Nothing good could possibly happen in a mangrove swamp.

CHAPTER 18

Half an hour later, I found myself at Walsh's café. I had volunteered to take his illegal coffee order to him. I hadn't yet investigated his girlfriend as a suspect. Madison certainly was suspicious on several points. She was Walsh's girlfriend, and Sheila's tearoom would have stood in direct opposition to Walsh's livelihood, but more so, she was top of my list for being a witch. She didn't live in town, but she visited it on occasion. That could explain why Sheila McFeeler had felt a witchy presence from time to time. I had no idea how I was going to question Walsh about his girlfriend. I planned to wing it.

I knocked at the back door of the café. Walsh opened the door and frowned.

"The retirement home residents sent me," I was quick to say.

His eyes opened wide in surprise.

"I have your delivery. Um, you know, Operation Room Service." *More like Broom Service, as I'm delivering it and I'm a witch*, I thought with a smile.

He looked around and then opened the door fully. "Come inside," he said in hushed tones.

I found myself in the kitchen. He beckoned to me and we walked through the kitchen and into what was clearly his office. It was small, with a big safe dominating the room. A small desk was pushed against one wall, and behind it was black office chair. I knew the type—it was one which required assembly. I had bought a similar one in Melbourne and had never quite figured how to assemble it. After I put it together, five pieces were left over, and it had collapsed the first time I had sat on it.

I turned my attention back to Walsh.

"I'll put it in a safe," he said, all the while looking nervously around.

When the coffee was safely locked away in the safe, he straightened up. "I suppose you have a lot of questions."

I scratched my head. "I must say, I found it

awfully strange. I couldn't believe the residents are dealing in illegal coffee. They have a whole production line going on."

"It was one of the nurses who came up with the idea," he told me. "The residents were horribly bored. Most of them used to have businesses of their own and they found their retirement boring. They were bored sitting around watching TV all day. The nurse told me that she got the idea from watching one of their shows."

"That was probably *Narcos*," I said, raising my eyebrows.

He nodded slowly. "I can easily buy coffee from the Gold Coast or Brisbane. Why, I can buy it at Ormeau just up the road, but I do it for the sake of the residents. Of course, it wouldn't do if I got caught."

"You know, I've been thinking about that," I said. "I wonder what would happen if someone did actually get caught with coffee. That would certainly test the law, wouldn't it?"

Walsh looked stricken. "Absolutely not! The lawyer I spoke to at length told me that it would certainly bring public attention to the issue, but he advised me very strongly against doing it."

I shrugged. "I see. Anyway, it's awfully kind of you to help the residents."

"I think it's quite funny, to tell you the truth," he said. "Who would think residents of a retirement home would be dealing in illegal coffee in Australia?"

We both chuckled, and then he said, "And can I offer you a coffee in exchange for delivering the illegal goods?"

"I'm a bit caffeine overloaded, but I will never say no to coffee. I can't believe the police haven't caught Sheila's killer yet!"

Walsh agreed. "Yes, that seems strange to me, too. East Bucklebury is a small town and there can't be many suspects."

"Maybe, it is someone who doesn't live here." I watched him closely.

He didn't seem to get my meaning. "Oh yes, a tourist." He nodded slowly as he spoke.

"What motive would a tourist have for murdering Sheila?"

He looked puzzled. "Yes, you're right," he said after an interval.

I was wondering how to mention Madison when my phone rang. It was Max. "Hello?" I said warily, hoping he didn't want me to do something with his parents, or rather, Tabitha.

It wasn't my day. "Goldie, how fast can you get to Walsh's café?"

"It won't take me long at all," I said. I omitted the fact that I was already there. "Why?"

"My parents and Tabitha will be there any minute, if they're not there already. I was supposed to meet them there. I invited you—didn't you get my text?"

I looked down at my phone. There were five missed calls from Max and a text asking me to meet him and his family at Walsh's café.

"I didn't see any of those," I said. "My phone has been annoying again. I have the sound turned up to high, but it's not notifying me of any texts. Your calls must have come when I was out of the car at the…" My voice trailed away.

Max did not appear to notice my lapse. "Well, I was going to have lunch with them all, but we have to question a suspect, and I'll be late. Could you go there and fill in for me, please?"

"Sure," I said. "You have another suspect?"

He simply thanked me and hung up.

The phone had been on loud, so Walsh overheard everything. "I'll bring a coffee out to your table, Goldie, and thanks your delivery." He winked at me.

I walked into the restaurant to see if Jack, Delilah, and Tabitha were there yet. If they weren't, I planned to rush home and change. After all, I had been in a mangrove swamp.

Unfortunately, the three of them were sitting at a table by the window with the good sea views. "You're never on time, are you!" Tabitha said by way of greeting.

I scowled at her. "Hello to you, too."

"You look dirty and grubby, not your usual plastic-coated self," Tabitha said.

"Hush, Tabitha!" Delilah looked horrified.

"Don't tell me what to do. You're just the first wife, but I'm the real wife."

Jack seemed oblivious to the exchange. I wondered how long Max would take. I certainly didn't want to referee Jack's wives, both past and present, although I was firmly on Delilah's side.

"I'm glad you could have lunch with us, Goldie," Jack said with a wide smile.

Walsh walked out and placed my coffee on the table. I was about to thank him when Tabitha said loudly, "Why did she get coffee first?"

"Goldie and I were speaking about a business matter moments ago," Walsh said firmly. "A waitress will be along to take your order soon." With that, he left.

"See that she is," Tabitha countered.

Delilah and I exchanged glances. I liked Max's parents, and wished I could have spent time with them away from Tabitha. I had never met a more obnoxious person. She was even more obnoxious than the most unpleasant clients I'd had back in Melbourne, and that was saying something.

Jack looked up from his newspaper. "It's good that Max has found another suspect. I wonder who it is?"

"It's probably Dolly. They questioned her husband, Boris, yesterday. I don't think there are any other suspects left, unless it was Sheila's son murdering her for the inheritance."

"Don't ever become a detective," Tabitha said with a snigger. "I'm sure it wasn't either of them."

I had been polite to her for the sake of Max, but now my patience was wearing thin. I turned to her. "So, do you know who did it? What's the name of *your* suspect?"

Her top lip curled up at the end, and then she looked away. She jabbed her stubby finger on the menu. "I'm having what I usually have. It's not as if there's much of a choice."

"Who do you think did it, Goldie?" Delilah asked me.

"A witch," I said without thinking.

Tabitha gasped, but Delilah simply said, "Yes, it would take a rather nasty person to murder a poor woman like that."

I agreed. I really had to think before I spoke from now on.

I looked around me but couldn't see Walsh within earshot. "There's also Walsh's girlfriend, Madison," I told them. "She works in marketing and she would have known how bad it was for Sheila to open a tearoom in town."

"Surely, there was a better motive than that," Jack said, but then he added, "But Goldie, you could be right. People get murdered for all sorts of strange reasons."

I looked up to see the waitress standing over us with pen and paper. "It's a terrible thing about Sheila's murder, isn't it?" We all nodded. She pushed on. "Did you know her well, Goldie?"

"I only spoke to her once or twice," I said.

"She was such good friends with your uncle,"

the waitress continued. "It's a wonder she didn't befriend you when you first moved to town."

I agreed. "Yes, I should have asked her... um, it's a pity I didn't get the opportunity to ask her why she didn't."

Then I remembered I also hadn't asked Sheila if she had a boyfriend. Even though I now thought the murderer was a witch, I still hadn't excluded the possibility that Sheila was having an affair and was murdered by a jealous wife.

While I was pondering this, the others were ordering. When it was my turn, I ordered and then said, "I've been trying to figure out who could have murdered Sheila. She wasn't having an affair, was she?"

The waitress shook her head. "No, absolutely not. We would have known about it if she had been. You're thinking she might have been murdered over an affair?"

"Yes," I admitted.

The waitress shook her head. "No, it had to be another reason."

She left, and Jack glanced at his paper. "Put that newspaper away. It's not polite to read it at the table when we're having lunch with you," Tabitha scolded him.

Jack had been looking at the sports page, but he flipped the paper over to the front to shut it. "Oh my goodness!" he exclaimed. "I can't believe it!

CHAPTER 19

"What is it?" I asked him.

He showed me the paper. "It's the poor woman who was murdered! Her photo is on the front page. We were in the café here and saw her having an argument with someone. That must have been just before she was murdered. You know, it must have been the very afternoon before. I didn't realise she was the woman who was murdered!"

"And that was when a sudden storm came up?" I asked. He nodded, but I pressed him to be certain. "I heard that Sheila came into this café and had an argument with a woman, and a thunderstorm with large hail suddenly came up at that time."

"Yes, that's right, isn't it dear?" Jack asked Tabitha.

She simply shrugged.

"That must have been the day before I flew up to the Gold Coast airport," Delilah said.

Jack turned to her. "Yes, that's right." To Tabitha, he said, "Surely, you remember it? We were sitting right here, eating, and she came in and yelled at someone, and then there was a violent thunderstorm completely out of nowhere."

"I had no idea you were in this café during that incident," I said to Jack. "Can you remember who else was in the restaurant?"

Jack looked blank. "No. Why, is it important?"

I thought quickly. "Maybe, the murderer was in the restaurant at the time. Do you know what Walsh's girlfriend, Madison, looks like?"

Jack shook his head.

I pulled out my phone and went onto the East Bucklebury Facebook community page. I scrolled through it, looking for photos of Walsh. It didn't take long before I found one of him with Madison. I showed it to Jack. "Is this her?"

"Yes, she was here at the time," he said.

I wondered where I could find a photo of Tristan to show him. It would have been interesting if Tristan was in the room at the time too. Madison and Tristan were the only two possible witch suspects I had, apart from the unknown which.

"It was far more crowded than it was today," Jack said.

"That's enough, Jack," Tabitha said.

Jack stopped speaking and nodded. Delilah and I exchanged glances. I could tell she thought that was uncharacteristic behaviour for him.

Suddenly, the penny dropped. I knew who the murderer was! I couldn't be positive, but I was almost certain.

But how could I prove it?

I forced a relaxed look onto my face. "Hopefully, Max is questioning the murderer right now and will make an arrest, and then the town can go back to normal," I said. I pulled out my phone and texted Oleander, telling her who I thought the murderer was, where I was, and what I planned to do.

I had to go home, get Persnickle, and take him back to Sheila's house. I needed to speak with Sheila and tell her my suspicions. Maybe, when I told her who I thought the murderer was, it might trigger a memory, or even a psychic sense. I was clutching at straws, but I was all out of options.

I excused myself and pretended I was going to the bathroom, but I slipped out the back door. "I'm going home to get something. Don't tell Max's relatives where I've gone if they happen to ask you," I said to Walsh.

He looked entirely puzzled, but simply said, "Sure."

I drove home through heavy rain. I wondered if the other sea witch caused it. Sure, there was a tropical cyclone west of Norfolk Island, but it wasn't supposed to make landfall for a couple of days, if at all.

I slipped into the house and locked the door behind me, and then went straight through to the kitchen to get Persnickle's leash. As I walked past him, he opened one eye and then went back to sleep. I grabbed his leash and headed back to him, just as there was a loud knock on the door.

I froze to the spot. What if it was the murderer? My heart beat out of my chest.

I stood there, hoping it was only Oleander and Athanasius, but they would have called out. Maybe, if I didn't answer the door, the murderer would go away, although my car was parked outside in full view.

Suddenly, at the same time as a deafening clap of thunder, the door flew open, and Tabitha was standing there.

"How did you know it was me?" she asked, as she stepped inside.

"For a start, you gasped when I said a witch did it," I said, "but the biggest giveaway was that you witnessed the argument Sheila had in Walsh's café. A sudden storm came out of nowhere at that time, and that would have tipped you off to the fact that Sheila was a sea witch."

"That's one of the reasons why I married that fool," she said. "The main reason was that Jack is very wealthy, of course, but I also knew his son lived in East Bucklebury, and East Bucklebury is famous in certain circles for attracting sea witches. I needed some powers."

"What did you need powers for?" I asked, genuinely curious.

She ran her hand up and down the length of her body, gesturing to herself. "Do you think this is natural? I can't look as good as this without witchcraft."

I bit back the ready retort. I certainly couldn't

say anything to antagonise her. I didn't know what powers she did, in fact, possess.

She was still speaking. "I'm really not eighty-two," she said. "I'm much, much older. It's just that stealing sea witches' powers gives me this youthful appearance."

Youthful appearance? Who was she kidding? Apart from herself, obviously.

"Let me get this straight," I said. "You came here to town looking for a sea witch?"

"Since I married Jack Grayson, I've come to town on occasion when he visits his son," she said. "I haven't found a sea witch until now. In fact, I wasn't even certain she was one until I suddenly got a burst of powers early that morning."

I held up one hand, palm outwards. "What? You killed her on the *off-chance* she was a sea witch?"

Tabitha nodded. "You can't take any chances at my age. I need all the help I can get. Botox and fillers can only get you so far."

"Yes, it all makes sense," I said. "You were the unknown witch."

"You're rambling," she snapped.

"Oleander, Athanasius, and I suspected Sheila's demise was at the hands of a witch rather than being a mundane murder, but we knew it couldn't be one of the town's residents. We knew it had to be someone who only visited on occasion. The only people we knew who visited on occasion were her son, Tristan, and Walsh's girlfriend, Madison. We also thought there could be a witch that we didn't know about."

Tabitha took another step towards me. "That would be me," she said.

"And I realised it was you when I heard you were in the café that day. I also thought how Jack seemed to be under your spell, and then I realised he was—he was literally under your spell. You put a spell on him."

"I always put a spell on men," she said with a dismissive wave of her hand. "Women should always put spells on men. That way, they do whatever you want."

I raised my eyebrows. "And it was you who made it rain at the protest rally, because you were annoyed I didn't stay at the picnic."

"Well, Miss Clever Pants, you won't have the chance to use my advice, because I'm going to do away with you right now." Lightning flashed behind her, framing her in the doorway.

What was it going to be? Weather wars? I certainly thought I could take her down.

That was when she pulled her orange handbag out from under her black raincoat and from it, produced a gun.

I heard a sound beside me and looked down. Persnickle opened one eye and then shut it, and then both eyes popped wide open. Tabitha advanced upon me, holding the gun higher. "Since Jack's stupid son, Max, is no closer to figuring out who did it, then they will think it's an unhinged serial killer," she said. "Plus I have an alibi. No one saw me leave the café, because I climbed out the bathroom window. I'll just climb back in. I told Jack I had an upset stomach, so he won't be surprised that I was away for so long. Goodbye, Goldie. I'd be lying if I said it was a pleasure knowing you."

As her finger closed on the trigger, Persnickle lunged at her orange handbag. He could sure move fast when he was angry.

It all happened in a flash. The gun went off, and bits of plaster fell on me from the ensuing hole in the ceiling. Tabitha must have dropped the gun in surprise, because it fell back into her orange handbag which Persnickle was currently attacking.

I ran over to get the gun, just as Max burst through the door.

"Your stepmother did it!" I said. "She's the murderer! She came here to kill me because I figured out she did it."

Tabitha was yelling obscenities, while trying to get the gun back out of her handbag. Max hurried over and snatched the gun. In one fluid motion he slapped handcuffs on her.

"How did you know it was her?" he asked me.

I bit my lip. I had to come up with a good answer on the spot. "I feel so faint from the shock," I said, and that was only a partial lie. "I was having lunch with them all like you asked me to, and your father saw a picture of Sheila McFeeler in the newspaper. He said that he and Tabitha had been in the café when Sheila came in and had the argument the day before she died. Tabitha got very angry when Jack repeated what Sheila had said. I thought it was strange that someone would get so upset over not being able to have coffee. That's when I began to suspect that she was the murderer. I texted Oleander and Athanasius and told them what I suspected. Then

I was going to drive to the police station to tell you."

Max narrowed his eyes. He was still hanging onto the struggling Tabitha. "Why didn't you just call me?"

"Because you were interviewing a witness, of course," I said. "I wanted to be there at the police station as soon as you finished questioning the suspect. So, I came home to get changed because I got caught in the rain earlier, as you can see. She came here to kill me."

"You're a terrible liar," Tabitha yelled at me. "No one would believe all that nonsense! No one in their right mind, at any rate."

"That's enough from you," Max said. "Goldie, are you all right?"

I fought the urge to run and throw my arms around his neck. He was still holding.to Tabitha.

"I'm all right for now, but I could do with a big hug later, as soon as you deal with her," I said.

CHAPTER 20

"Hi, Lucifer." Max's voice was warm. He scooped the cat off the kitchen counter and scratched him behind the ear. "You're not terrorising poor Persnickle, are you?"

I laughed as I lured my wombat out from the pantry with a packet of treats. Lucifer had chased him in there earlier, determined to play rough. That cat was as bad as his namesake. Okay, not as bad, but certainly naughty. Max had brought him over in an attempt to get him used to Persnickle.

"I wish I could have kept the kitty, but I don't think Persnickle would have been too impressed with that." I scratched the wombat on his bottom as he eyed Lucifer warily. The two were never going to be friends.

"I'm glad I kept him," Max replied as Lucifer purred loudly. Max was the only person the cat liked. "I didn't want him to go to the pound."

"I didn't want that either," I admitted.

"Sorry about all the fuss." Jack stuck his head around the kitchen door. "I had no idea Tabitha was so…"

"Deranged?" said Max.

"Scary?" I offered. "Criminally insane?"

Delilah followed Jack into the kitchen. "You used to have much better taste in women," she said to Jack, her fingers lingering on the finger where her wedding band had lived for so many years. "Much, much better taste."

"I agree," Max said, and Lucifer purred even louder.

"Should we pop a bottle of champagne to celebrate?" Delilah said then.

"What are we celebrating?" I asked.

"Jack's divorce."

We laughed as Delilah carried a tray of glasses into the garden. I rummaged through the fridge. I couldn't find any champagne, but I did find two bottles of wine. It was fortunate that Delilah had taken the whole tray, because Oleander and

Athanasius turned up as soon as Max had opened the bottle.

"What are we celebrating?" Oleander asked, which made everyone laugh again.

Jack slipped his wedding ring off his finger and tossed into the garden, which made everyone cheer. Everyone except Max, who sank into a chair and rested his chin in the palm of his hands.

"What's wrong?" I asked, sitting in the chair beside him.

"I just didn't know Tabitha loved coffee *that* much," he replied quietly.

"What do you mean?" I asked before I could stop myself.

"I mean, who knew she loved coffee enough to kill over it? An innocent woman has died, thanks to Tabitha's coffee addiction. Couldn't she have just switched to drinking tea? She was only visiting for a few days."

"Tea and coffee are two very different drinks." I wasn't about to spill the beans—coffee or otherwise—to Max about why Tabitha really killed Sheila. That was a conversation for another time.

"Why did you two break up in the first place?" Oleander was saying to Jack and Delilah. "You both seem so compatible."

Jack sighed. "I'm an idiot."

Delilah readily agreed. "Yes, but I knew that when I married you. I guess love just fades sometimes."

"And sometimes it returns," Jack said softly.

I raised an eyebrow at Max, who grinned. His parents reuniting would certainly lift his mood. I wondered if we could somehow lock them in a cupboard together. Or strand them at sea in a boat.

"I forgot something in the kitchen," I said as I rose. "And so did Max. And Oleander. And Athanasius."

"What could we have all possibly left in the…" Athanasius suddenly grabbed his leg. "Ouch! Oh."

I had the sneaking suspicion that Oleander had kicked him in the ankle. The four of us, along with Lucifer and a grumpy Persnickle, retreated into the kitchen. It was in the kitchen that we all stood with our faces pressed against the window, watching Jack and Delilah talk.

"Put on some music," I whispered to Max. "Something romantic."

Max hurried out of the room. Athanasius took the opportunity to address me. "If it wasn't for

Operation Room Service, you would never have caught the killer."

I was puzzled. "How do you figure you that?"

"It was one set of circumstances that led to another," he said sagely. "You made the delivery to Walsh, and it was in Walsh's café that you figured out Tabitha was the murderer."

"There are more holes in that argument than in a sieve," Oleander protested. She caught my arm and nodded as the sound of Elton John drifted out of the house into the garden.

I looked out the window and studied Jack and Delilah's faces. For a moment, they looked startled, and then Jack took Delilah into his arms. They were dancing. Athanasius went to hoot with delight, but Oleander clapped a hand over his mouth.

"Don't ruin the moment, old man," she said.

Athanasius chuckled. Then he took Oleander into his arms and started to dance. I thought Oleander would look upset, but she was absolutely delighted. It turns out the pair knew quite a few moves. I imagined them at my age, dancing through the twilit streets. It was a nice image. A nice image that I did not get to see for too long, because Max had other ideas.

He placed the still purring Lucifer on the kitchen table, told him to behave, and then took me into his arms. Persnickle didn't seem all too pleased that his new nemesis was free, but I didn't have time to worry about my wombat. We were slow dancing to Elton John. Max and I! I tried not to blush as I felt the warmth of Max's hand through my cotton dress. I wish I had worn something other than these shoes. Like my heels.

Why was I never prepared for a romantic moment? If Max and I ever got engaged, I'd probably have my hair in curlers, a green mask slathered all over my face, and spinach in my teeth.

I needed to act calm, but the lighting was too intense in the kitchen. It would show off every flaw in my face. Ordinarily, I wouldn't mind, but Max was holding me in his arms. Trying to act normal, I slow danced Max over to the light switch and knocked it off with my elbow.

Suddenly, the kitchen was filled with a romantic light. It was the kind of blue light that occurs when the sun has set but night has not yet risen.

"Is it a little dark?" Max whispered in my ear.

I grinned to myself. "Oops. Must have hit the light. How clumsy."

Max didn't say anything. He pressed his lips against my forehead as I closed my eyes. *Would it be so bad to stand in this man's arms forever?* I asked myself. I was safe here. And warm.

ABOUT MORGANA BEST

USA Today Bestselling author Morgana Best survived a childhood of deadly spiders and venomous snakes in the Australian outback. Morgana Best writes cozy mysteries and enjoys thinking of delightful new ways to murder her victims.

www.morganabest.com